TWO
ThE
HaRD
WaY

TWO
ThE
HaRD
WaY

TRAVIS HUNTER

KENSINGTON PUBLISHING CORP.
www.kensingtonbooks.com

DAFINA BOOKS are published by

Kensington Publishing Corp.
119 West 40th Street
New York, NY 10018

All Kensington titles, imprints, and distributed lines are available at special quantity discounts for bulk purchases for sales promotion, premiums, fund-raising, educational, or institutional use.

Special book excerpts or customized printings can also be created to fit specific needs. For details, write or phone the office of the Kensington Special Sales Manager: Kensington Publishing Corp., 119 West 40th Street, New York, NY 10018. Attn. Special Sales Department. Phone: 1-800-221-2647.

Dafina and the Dafina logo Reg. U.S. Pat. & TM Off.

ISBN-13: 978-0-7582-4250-1
ISBN-10: 0-7582-4250-6

First Printing: August 2010
10 9 8 7 6 5 4 3 2 1

Printed in the United States of America

*This book is dedicated to the memory of
my great-grandparents Rosa and James Charles.*

Acknowledgments

Working with young adults has been my calling for the last ten years. As I traveled the country touring with my adult novels, I made it a point to always stop by a high school, youth center, or library where I could speak with teenagers about how important it is to make good choices. As I made those stops, parents would always come up to me and ask if I had anything their teenager could read. Although my adult novels are not as over the top as some of the things that are out there, I never felt comfortable suggesting something that I wrote for adults. However, I couldn't think of any other novel to suggest, so I wrote my own.

I would like to thank God for all of His blessings; my son, Rashaad Hunter, for being the best kid in the entire world; Linda Hunter, for being the best mother a guy could ask for; Dr. Carolyn Rogers, for always encouraging me to reach for the stars; Carrie Moses, Sharon Capers, Andrea and David Gilmore, Lynette Moses, James (Ray Ray) Moses, Amado and Hunter Rogers, Barry Moses, Ron Gregg, Ahmed, Ayinde, Shani, Jabade and Louis Johnson, Mary and Willard Jones, Monica (Imani) McCullough, and all of the wonderful book clubs who read my novels; my agent, Sara Camilli, and my editor, Selena James, for making this happen; and Melody Guy, for getting this started.

PROLOGUE
ROMEO

I paced the rooftop of my apartment complex with a .40-caliber Glock pistol in the palm of my hand, sweat pouring off of my closely cropped head. Fear had a stranglehold on me, and my heart threatened to beat its way out of my chest. I struggled to control my breathing as I eased over to the edge of the building and took in the sight of the only place I had ever called home. That's when I realized that life as I knew it was over.

A nervous chuckle escaped my lips. How dare I ever allow myself to dream of a life outside of this box I was placed in since the day I was born? First my brother's dreams were snatched away, then mine. The more I thought about it, the more I realized my life was doomed from the start.

1

ROMEO

"You ever cheated on Ngiai?" my best friend, Amir, asked me as we walked home from school on a wooded path toward our home in the busted-in and burned-out subsidized projects. Atlanta's Village Apartments had been my home for the last ten years of my life, and although it was a pretty rough spot, I liked it.

"Who is that?" I smiled.

"Whatever. You a player but you ain't stupid."

"I don't cheat. I'm a good boy," I said.

"Man," Amir said, shaking his head. "How you function with all those girls up in your face all the time?"

"The same way you function with none in your face. I just keep it moving."

"What? You crazy. I got more than my share of the honeys, player. I just keep my business to myself," Amir said.

"Yeah, that's not all you keep to yourself. But you should embrace your virginity and stop being ashamed of it."

"You crazy. I lost my virginity a long time ago, lil buddy," Amir bragged his lie.

"Yeah, but Fancy and her four sisters don't count," I said, wiggling my fingers in his face.

"Whatever, homie," he said, smacking my hand down. "Like I said, I keep mine's to myself. I'm respectful of the woman I spend my private time with. Don't need to run around here telling you low-self-esteem-having clowns 'bout my business."

"Yeah, okay," I said.

"What the . . . ," Amir said, stopping in his tracks as we noticed the path to our apartments was cut off by a six-foot-high wrought-iron fence.

"I guess we're moving on up, Amir," I said, running my fingers along the black iron. "I always wanted to live in a gated community."

Amir folded his arms. His face wore a disgusted scowl. He was quiet and his breathing was measured. He seemed to be analyzing the situation we had before us. One of the men working on the gate nodded at me and I nodded back.

"Don't be speaking to no Mexicans, Romeo," Amir snapped. He huffed a frustrated breath, then found his stride along the fence line. "Those people are the worst of the worst. The white man tells them to put up a fence locking black folks in and they jump on the job. No standards. Anything for a buck," Amir said. "You don't see what's going on?"

Amir kept me laughing. He was a walking worrywart who believed the government was secretly conspiring to eliminate the black man from the face of the earth. Maybe that was the reason his hair was turning gray at the tender age of seventeen. He claimed his dad was a political prisoner, but in reality he was just a prisoner who got caught selling drugs.

"Nah, why don't you tell me what's going on, Reverend Al Sharpton Jr.?" I said.

"This is nothing more than the government's way of preparing us for incarceration. My daddy sent me a book, and he said the only reason they call where we live the 'projects' is because the powers that be are doing a project on how to eliminate our black butts."

"Your daddy's a genius, dude. You are so lucky that he imparts such deep wisdom on the world," I said sarcastically. "That's why they keep him locked up, man. He's too smart to unleash on the world."

"Okay, see, you think this is a game. You're one of those dum-dums who can't call a spade a spade. I can't believe you can't see what's going on, Romeo. They tryna condition us to being surrounded by fences. And what does a prison have? A bunch of doggone gates." He looked at me like I was the dumbest person ever to take a breath. "That's what's wrong with black people. We don't think."

"So now you got a problem with black people too?"

His eyes almost popped out of his head. "My *biggest* problem is with black people. We the worst of the worst."

"I thought you just said Mexicans were the worst of the worst."

"Hell . . . neither one of us are worth a red cent. But I'll tell you what—black people are the only group of people on this earth who just don't care how we look on TV. We're just happy to be on TV. Master want me to play a pimp and degrade my sisters . . . Okay." He mocked a wide-eyed minstrel character. "They be like, 'You ain't even gotta pay me that much—just put me on TV so people can think I'm somebody and I'll beat that ho to death.'"

I laughed as I always did when Amir went off on one of his race tangents.

"Now, I will say one thing about Mexicans," he said. "They will work."

"Black people work too," I defended. "This country was built on the backs of black people."

"Man, that was three hundred years ago. And we ain't done jack since. I guess we're resting."

"What about Barack Obama?"

"Man, whatever. One man out of two million and you want me to jump up and clap."

"Shut up, Amir," I said.

"I'm just saying," Amir said, sticking his middle finger up at a big poster of a fancy-dressed real estate mogul whose face was plastered on the side of a MARTA bus station. "We done lost all of our pride, man. There's nothing sacred in the black community anymore."

"Why do you stick your finger up at that picture every day?" I asked.

"Do you know who that is?"

"Nope," I said.

"Damn, Rome. You gotta get a little more involved in something other than rap videos and SportsCenter. That's the fool who owns all of these apartment complexes around here. Mr. Slumlord himself. He's riding around in Bentleys and we living in the hood. I don't have a problem with him getting paid, but I do have a problem if he's getting paid from keeping us poor."

"Now, in all of your extensive research, how did you find out that keeping us in the hood makes him rich?"

Amir shook his head again. "It's a good thing you can throw a football, because you 'bout one stupid little boy."

"Enlighten me, Dr. Know-It-All."

Amir shook his head. "Lord, I swear my people are going to perish due to stupidity. The government pays big money to people who take on section eight and subsidize housing. Damn Democrats."

"So you are a Republican, Amir?"

"Not really, I'm Amir. The government is full of crap."

"Shut up, Amir."

"That man on that poster is no different than those slave catchers who used to chase down other blacks for the plantation owner."

"You can find a way to compare everything to slavery," I said, growing tired of Amir's Black Panther moment.

"Okay, name one thing that we as black folks can't find a joke about."

I searched my brain but couldn't come up with anything.

"I'm telling you, Rome. You can think about it until your black face turns blue, but you ain't coming up with nothing. We laugh about everything, a hee hee hee. Even slavery. I bet you won't find a Jewish person laughing about the Holocaust."

"How you gonna judge an entire race based on a few clowns?" I said, getting pulled back in again.

My boy Amir was a character, and I loved getting him riled up. All five-foot-two inches of him. He had a caramel-brown complexion and a big gray patch of hair in the middle of his head. He gave me that Boo Boo the Fool look again.

"We allow those clowns to prosper. We celebrate these fools and make 'em spokespeople for the black community. Have you ever seen the Ying Yang Twins? What about Gucci Mane?"

I had to laugh at that one.

"And that's who we have representing us. I rest my case," he said, throwing his hands up in the air.

"You know, Amir, you should've been born in the fifties or sixties so you could really have something to complain about."

"Oh, you think it's all gravy now, Mr. Dumb Football Player? Racism worse now than it was in the sixties, only now they don't wear white sheets—they wear suits. That's because they're the CEOs of the record labels and television stations. That includes the black CEOs too. If they really gave a hoot about helping blacks, then they wouldn't go and find the most ignorantiest people they can find and put them on TV for little kids to look up to. I swear, I wish I could go on a Nat Turner spree and get away with it."

"*Ignorantiest?* That's not even a word. And you got the nerve to call me dumb."

"It's these public schools, man," Amir said, shaking his head. "But you know what I mean."

Our low-level political debate came to a halt when we saw a few of the project natives standing around a fancy car belonging to a neighborhood hustler name Pete "Wicked" Sams.

Wicked had a few of the locals' undivided attention as he told tall tales of his life as an outlaw. He stopped mid-sentence when he saw me.

"Romey Rome," Wicked called, waving his arm for me to come over and join him. "Holla at me."

"What's up, Wicked?" I said, throwing my hand up in the air and not missing a stride. I knew better. Wicked would have me out there with him all day long talking about what he used to do on the football field. The more he told the story, the better a player he became, and I had heard it so much that by now, to hear him tell it, he was better than every player in the NFL.

"Come here, boy," Wicked called out, which was more like a command.

"I'm in a hurry, man," I said, slowing a little.

"You in too much of a hurry that you can't come and holla at your boy?" Wicked said, playing the guilt card.

Amir shot me a look and shook his head.

"Man, let me go and holla at this fool for a minute," I said, finally relenting.

"You go right ahead. I ain't about to sit up here all day listening to some fool who calls himself Wicked," Amir said. "I'm going home to handle some business."

"A'ight, man. I'll see you later," I said.

"Rock on, black man," Amir said, throwing up his peace sign as he hurried to his building.

"Where the militant midget running off to?" Wicked asked me as I walked over to him and gave him a fraternity-brother-like hug.

"Home, I guess," I said, shaking a few more hands.

"So are you sitting on the bench, or you getting in the game?"

"Don't even try me like that," I said. "How's life treating you, Pete?"

"Beating me down, but hey," Wicked said, rubbing his ample stomach. "I'm eating good."

"I see," I said, eyeing the Buddha-like thing hanging on the front of his body. "You look like you're about six months pregnant."

A few of the flunkies laughed but quickly zipped their lips when Wicked jerked his head in their direction.

"What you do last game?" Wicked asked, turning back to me.

"Threw for two hundred and ran for a hundred but we lost, so it didn't matter."

"Damn, boy, you the high school all world, ain't cha?"

"Nah, just doing me," I said.

"Keep doing what you doing. I be hearing about cha. You got a lil buzz going round. You know I blew my career up hanging out here in these damn streets. I'm telling you, Rome, I used to be a beast." Wicked's eyes widened with excitement.

Here we go, I thought to myself.

"Ray Lewis ain't had nothing on me, boy. I used to break bones. Crack! I'm talking about giving coaches straight up sleepless nights tryna figure out how to block me. Had lil quarterbacks like you in straight panics. Rome, I would've broke you up, boy."

"You too slow, Wicked," I said, shaking my head. "You wouldn't stand a chance."

"You crazy. Ask your brother 'bout me, boy. Matter of fact, come by the crib. I got tapes to prove my word ain't a lie."

"Whatever. I don't wanna see any tapes. If you were all that, then why ain't you in the league?"

"See, my problem was I wanted that fast money."

Wicked spread his arms and nodded toward his black 745 BMW. "Ain't doing too bad but if I could do it all again, I might've paid for this ride with different dollars."

"It's not too late," I said.

"Look at you. Mr. Opportunistic. Always looking on the bright side."

"You mean *optimistic.*"

"That's what I said."

"No, you said *opportunistic.*"

Wicked turned to one of his flunkies. "What did I say?"

"You said it right," said Mark, a tall skinny kid whose only job on earth was to be Wicked's yes-man.

"Whatever," I said. "How are you gonna ask somebody who failed pre-K to answer a question about a word with more than one syllable?"

"Who you talking to?" Mark said, puffing out his little birdlike chest and yanking the chain of his vicious-looking pit bull.

"You," I said, not in the least bit concerned with him or his dog.

"Mark, shut yo mouth, boy. We can't have Romeo out here hurting up his hands on the likes of you," Wicked said, pushing his flunky away.

"I ain't worried about his hands. I'ma let this damn dog go on him."

"I'm petrified," I said. "Oh, my bad. That's three syllables. I meant to say, I'm scared."

"Come on, Rome." Wicked went into his boxer's stance. "I'm tired of you and all *your* mouth."

I still didn't move. Pete was my older brother Kwame's friend, so he looked at me as if I was his little brother. That was the only reason I could get away with talking to him the way I did. Anyone else would be picking up a few teeth right about now.

"Boy, how old is you now?" Wicked asked.

"Seventeen."

"And you what?" Wicked stood in front of me and placed his hand at his head to measure who was the tallest. "Six feet."

"Six-one," I said, standing up. "You know my brother might be coming home in a few days. His parole hearing's tomorrow."

"Aw, man." Wicked swatted away my concern with his chubby hand. "That lil crack charge ain't 'bout nuttin'. Ain't no *might* about it—he coming home. And you tell him I said come holla at me the minute he touches town."

"I can't wait for him to get out of that place. He's been gone too long," I said, thinking about how much I missed the guy who was far more than a big brother to me. He was also the only father figure I'd ever had. Everything I knew, I learned it from Kwame.

"Two years." Wicked frowned up his face. "Man, that ain't jack. I can do that without a snack."

"Two years is a long time."

"For you maybe, but not for my dog. See you . . . Big Nana sheltered you too much. Wouldn't let you cuss, made you do your homework, and had you up in piano lessons like you was gonna be a black Rocketeer or somebody," Wicked said, drawing laughter from his cronies.

"There you go. I'm outta here," I said, reaching out to tap his fist with mine.

"A'ight. Tell Kwame I said come holla at a player when he gets himself settled," Wicked said, touching his heart.

"Okay," I said, walking away and frowning at the ludicrous thought of my brother putting himself back into the same situation that got him arrested in the first place. I wasn't sure what led to his arrest, because everyone kept the details from me, but I was almost one hundred percent sure Wicked had something to do with it.

"Rome." Wicked stood and shuffled his three-hundred-pound frame over to me. "Hold up, boy. You always rushing off somewhere." He placed a roll of money in my palm.

"What's this for?"

"Just a lil something something. Make sure Kwame knows I gave you that. If . . . When he gets home, give him some of it and tell him I said we need to talk."

I nodded and we shared another brotherly hug.

Living in the Village Apartments, aka "The V," gave you an edge, a hardness that was essential if you were going to survive the everyday rigors of life in subsidized housing. But it was also a trap waiting to close its jaws around you at the slightest slipup. I made my way through the breezeways between the buildings and stopped when I saw General Mack, our neighborhood nutcase and shell-shocked war veteran, marching a line of five-year-olds as if they were in basic training.

"Hut two, three, four. Pick ya legs up, soldier. Hey, pay attention, boy. You gonna mess around and get yourself shot," he sang with all seriousness.

"Good Lord. That man is nuttier than a fruitcake," I said, shaking my head at the spectacle before me. The kids seemed to be having fun, so all I could do was laugh before heading upstairs to the apartment I shared with my nana.

2

ROMEO

"Nana," I called out the second I crossed the thresh-
old into our small, two-bedroom apartment.

"Boy, please hush all that fuss," Nana said with a frown.
Beatrice "Nana" Braxton was as beautiful as the day was
long. Heavyset, with gray hair that came down to the small
of her back and sweet as a peach cobbler. The woman we
all called Nana was sitting at her sewing machine making a
quilt when she stopped what she was doing to chastise
me.

I took a whiff of the air and knew right away that we
had company. An old green army jacket was draped over
the arm of the sofa. My eyes darted around the room,
looking for the one person I could go the rest of my life
without seeing. I found her walking out of the bathroom,
rubbing her hands on a pair of dirty cargo pants.

"Hey, Romeo," she said, brushing imaginary lint from
an equally dirty denim shirt.

I nodded but didn't utter a word.

"You can't speak to your momma?" Nana said, pulling herself to her feet with a grunt. She walked over to me and placed a hand on the small of my back. "Go on and give your momma a hug," she said with a nudge.

"I spoke," I said, not moving toward the haggard-looking woman with whom I shared my big brown eyes, pointy nose, and full lips.

"I know I'm old, but I didn't know I was hard of hearing," Nana said.

Reluctantly, I walked over to my scraggly-looking mother and gave her a halfhearted hug. The stench coming from her body almost choked the life out of me. She smelled like something had crawled up inside of her and died.

"How you doing, Pearl?" I said. I had abandoned the "Mommy" tag shortly after she abandoned us.

"I'm doing good. I got a job." She smiled her lie with stained and plaque-caked teeth. "Things are about to change for me, Romeo. But I'm just taking it one day at a time."

"Um-huh," I grunted.

Seeing my mother broke my heart all over again. It also brought back memories of how I felt ten years ago when I was teased relentlessly by the neighborhood kids when they saw her storming up and down the street in a drug-induced high, screaming, "Dirty Harry, Dirty Harry, Dirty Harry. I'ma get you. Dirty Harry, Dirty Harry, Dirty Harry, I'ma get you." She would yell this at the top of her lungs, over and over, at her imaginary enemies. The police would arrest her for disorderly conduct or harassment, but a few days later, she would be out of jail and right back at it again with her Dirty Harry rant.

"You look so good," she said, eyeing me from my head

to my toes. She reached out to touch me, but I pulled away. She seemed to think better of it, anyway, and pulled her hand back. I gave her a once-over to let her know that I couldn't say the same about her.

"I bet you driving those little girls crazy round here. That's one thing about me—I don't make no ugly babies. Where's Kwame?"

I turned to Nana, asking with my eyes how much longer I had to endure this foolishness. She nodded her head that I had been respectful long enough.

"Nana, did you eat anything today?" I asked, turning away from my mother as if she had disappeared.

"Boy, you know ain't nothing in that icebox. My check didn't come today—maybe it'll show up tomorrow—so if you're hungry, you gonna have to make do with what's in the cabinets."

"I asked you if you ate."

"And I told you ain't nothing in the icebox. I had some soup."

I walked back toward my bedroom but kept my eye on my mother. "I got some money. You can go to the grocery store if you feel like it."

Pearl cleared her throat at the mention of money.

"No, I don't feel like doing much of anything. I tried to call Dr. James, but her secretary or somebody put me on hold," Nana said. "I guess she forgot about me, 'cause she sho never came back to the phone. You think you can call her?"

"What's wrong?" I asked, walking back out to the living room. "You said they put you on hold and never came back?"

She fanned away my concern. "Nothing to worry about. Just been feeling tired lately."

I didn't like the sound of that. Nana was everything to me, and I didn't know what I would do if something happened to her.

"Momma, you been taking your medication?" Pearl asked only after reading my concern. "Your blood pressure still high?"

"I'm fine." Nana wrinkled up her nose. "Pearl, why don't you go in that bathroom and clean yourself up? Take you a shower and let me wash those clothes for you."

"I can't. I gotta run. I told you I was working, and I don't want to be late. I just came by to check in on y'all." She smiled, showing those pathetic-looking teeth that made me want to throw up.

"Do you have time to brush your teeth?" I asked.

She quickly closed her mouth and looked at the floor. I could see the hurt that I caused written all over her face.

Every time I saw my mother, I couldn't help but remember the days when she took pride in her appearance and took even more pride in being a mother.

Kwame and I would almost attack her the minute she walked through the door from a hard day of work at the construction site where she labored side by side with men twice her size. We would shove a football, a basketball, or a baseball in her face and beg her to play with us. We thought we had the coolest mom in the world. She played basketball, had run track in high school, and had lots of newspaper articles covering her accomplishments.

Back in those early days, she would never complain about being tired. She would put her tool bag down and come outside and play with her boys. After about an hour with us, she would throw up her hands and head into the house to cook a fabulous meal. Once the streetlights came on, she would expect to hear us walk through the door and wash up for dinner. Then one day, out of the blue, Nana came and picked us up. We moved in with her, and it was as if Pearl had just disappeared. A few months later, she showed up looking like death itself. After that, she would pop up once or twice a year looking worse than she did the last time we saw her. I used to ask Nana all the time what was going on with her, but all she would do was shake her head and fight off the tears, so eventually I stopped asking.

"When will we know something about Kwame?" Nana asked me.

"Yeah," Pearl said. "What's he up to?"

I ignored her and turned to Nana. "He said the counselors said his chances are good. So we'll see. I'm headed up to talk to his lawyer in a few."

Nana sighed heavily. "My heart can't take sitting around waiting to see if some stranger who don't know nothing about nothing is gonna give my boy what should be rightfully his in the first place."

"Don't worry about it, Nana," I said. "He'll be alright. Here's some money in case you decide to go to the grocery store."

"Where you get money from?" she asked with a skeptical look on her face.

"My football coach gave me a few dollars for tutoring his son," I said, peeling off a twenty-dollar bill from the roll Wicked gave me. I hated lying to Nana, but she didn't care too much for Wicked or his wicked ways.

"Good for you. You always was a smart boy." She smiled proudly.

I glanced over and noticed Pearl hungrily eyeing my money. I slid the rest back into my pocket and walked to my bedroom.

I closed the door behind me and looked over at the empty bed by the window. Nana told me I could take it down after my brother was sent off to prison, but I couldn't bring myself to do it. I guess I felt if I took it down, I was accepting that he wasn't coming back for a while.

I hurried out of my warm-up suit with the words TUCKER FOOTBALL stenciled across the front. I went to the closet and pulled out the only suit I owned. I hoped it would still fit. The last time I wore it was over a year ago.

"Why you puttin' on ya Sunday clothes?" Pearl asked as she eased into my bedroom. "Where are you going?"

"I gotta go and talk to Kwame's lawyer."

"Lawyer? What kind of lawyer Kwame got?"

"A criminal lawyer," I snapped. "He's in prison."

"Prison." Pearl frowned and placed a hand over her heart. "What did he do?"

"Nothing. He's probably coming home soon," I said, holding the pants up in front of me. They were a little bit short. I placed them back into the closet. Couldn't do the Andre 3000 look today. I grabbed another pair of pants and slid into them.

"But," she said with a sad face, "where is he?"

Part of me wanted to tell her everything. How our lives had been turned upside down when she left, but then I quickly decided against it. She wasn't in any condition to talk about anything relevant.

"No place."

"Where is no place? Every place is someplace. Do you want me to go with you?"

"Ah, no, thank you. Besides, we wouldn't want you to be late for work," I said, patronizing her.

I could tell she knew I knew she was lying. She also knew I was trying to be hurtful by exposing her, and for some strange reason, I regretted doing that.

"Yeah," she said, forcing a smile. "You're right."

I slid my feet into a pair of shoes that were too tight. "I gotta game tomorrow night. You should try to make it," I said, attempting to make up for my stab at her.

"Yeah," she said, walking all the way into my room. She looked around a few times, then plopped her funky butt down on my bed. "That would be nice. Baseball, right?"

I jumped up and almost fell back down because my feet were killing me. I didn't have another pair of shoes, and I didn't want to show up at a place of business rocking my Air Forces, so I sucked it up. I maneuvered my feet as best I could in the tight loafers. Didn't help, but I was going to have to deal with it.

"Nah, football, but I gotta get outta here," I said. "I wear number one, just in case you make it."

"I wouldn't miss it," she said, and for a second she reminded me of the mother I used to know. "Hey, Romeo."

"Yeah," I said, turning around to face her.

"You think you could . . ." She paused, seeming to search for the right words.

I knew what was coming next.

"You think you could let me hold a few dollars until I get paid? I get my check on Monday. I just need enough to get me something to eat and bus fare."

"I got a bus pass you can have, and if you wanna walk with me, I can get you something to eat."

Her smile turned upside down, and an incredible metamorphosis took place right before my eyes. Her eyes turned a deep bloodshot red and they narrowed into little slits. I could literally see the beast coming out of her.

"Just give me the damn money, boy," she said in a low growl. Her hands were clenched at her sides.

"No," I said flatly, although I was amazed at what I saw before me.

She reached for my pocket, and I grabbed her hand.

"I need this money, Romeo," she said.

"I gotta go," I said, tossing her hand away from my pockets. "You should get you some help. But if you're hungry, my offer still stands."

Her entire mood shifted. It was as if my kindness softened her.

"Romeo, your momma done come a long way, but I still got a long road to travel, you know. I need you to help me out a little bit. Just a few dollars would help me a lot. I'm trying to get it together, but these things take time. Just give me a few dollars. Please," she begged.

"Sorry, Pearl," I said, fighting myself to not give her the money. The part of me that refused to contribute to her demise won.

The beast came back. She huffed and puffed and looked like she wanted to blow my head off. She reached for me again, but I grabbed her hands and easily pried them away from me.

"Keep your hands off of me," I said in a firm voice.

"I'm sorry, son. I . . . I . . . I am," she said, blinking her eyes rapidly as if trying to shake the demons off.

I stood there for a few seconds, staring at the woman who had comforted me through my childhood aches and pains, and all I could do was shake my head. I left my room and went out to the living room where Nana was sitting on the sofa. I walked over and kissed her on the forehead. When I stood back up, I saw Pearl staring at me.

Something was definitely wrong with her, but I wasn't qualified enough to figure it out, so I turned away and tried to forget her.

"Nana, don't let her take anything from my room," I said.

"I didn't raise any thieves, Romeo," Nana chastised me with a sharp look.

"Okay," I said, my eyes on Pearl, who was standing by my door giving me the evil eye. "I'll call you on my way back to see what you want to eat."

"That's fine," Nana said, letting me know she was disappointed in me.

Pearl stormed toward us, grabbed her jacket, and walked out of the apartment without saying a word to me or Nana. I thought I saw a tear rolling down her face. I wasn't sure how I felt about it. After all, she was still my mother.

3

ROMEO

I ran toward the corner where I normally caught the bus and was stopped dead in my tracks by that brand-new fence.

I gotta get used to that thing, I thought.

I could see the MARTA bus making its way toward me, and if I walked around the fence, then I was sure to miss it, so I had to jump it. I couldn't get any traction in my slippery dress shoes, and the bus was steadily barreling toward me. I reached up and grabbed the top of the fence to pull myself over it.

Ouch!

The pointed side of the fence stuck me in the hand, drawing blood. I almost fell back down, but I made it across. I grimaced in pain, held my bloody hand with my good one, and ran to the bus stop. The big vehicle came to a halt and I got on, showed my bus pass to the driver, and plopped down in the front seat. I looked down at my hand and saw that the bleeding wasn't so bad. It was just a flesh cut, but it still could use a little attention. I leaned over and asked the driver if he had anything for my hand. He looked back and nodded toward a first-aid kit hanging by the token collector.

"Do I just get it myself?"

"You want me to stop the bus and get it?" he asked sarcastically as he whipped the big steering wheel around and turned onto Highway 78, headed toward downtown Decatur.

"I didn't want to assume," I said, standing up and retrieving the kit. I opened it and grabbed some gauze and a mini bottle of peroxide. After cleaning and wrapping my hand, I closed the kit and put it back where I'd found it. "Thanks, man," I said.

"That ain't your throwing hand, is it?" the driver asked. He was a funny-looking man. Gray hair with a bald spot showing a shiny dome, but the funny thing was he had a ponytail covered with colorful rubber bands.

"Nah," I said, surprised that the man knew who I was.

"Y'all looked good the other night. Just ain't got no defense. You did your job, but who in the hell y'all got back there playing cornerback?"

I smiled, then laughed. My man Amir was the culprit.

"That boy couldn't catch a cold in Alaska if all he had on was tighty whities and a fedora. What in the world was y'all coach thinking about when he put that joker in the game?"

I laughed at the visual. "We're working on him," I said.

"Four passes landed in his hands and what did he do? Dropped all four of them. I mean, come on, man. Put him on the bench with some Krazy Glue on his butt. That boy is a disgrace to the game."

"He's fast, so we need the speed," I said, still laughing at the old man and his high-pitched New Orleans accent. "And our starter was suspended for failing some classes."

"Speed? Well, he needs to use that speed to hurry up and find somewhere to sit his butt down. Maybe he should take up badminton, swimming, or something, but I swear football ain't his thing."

"I hear ya," I said.

"You know where you going to college at yet?"

"Not yet. Still tryna figure it out," I said, still amazed that so many people were concerned about my choice of college.

"Let me give you a piece of advice, son. Leave. Too many distractions around here for you. Young folks round here shooting each other just 'cause they mad. In my day, a good fistfight was good enough to settle a problem, but not these days. Youngins these days can't fight. Scared to take a beat-down. Would rather shoot somebody and go to prison than deal with a lil embarrassment. Signs that the end is near."

"I'll keep that in mind," I said. "This is my stop right here."

He pushed the brakes, and the bus squeaked to a halt. "Boy, I'll tell you, Fred Flintstone got better brakes than this doggone bus," he said.

"It was nice talking to you, my man," I said, standing up and waiting on the five or six people who sat behind me to exit the bus.

"You too. Keep your head on straight and you'll make something out of yourself," he said. "And always be your own man. Be selfish with your life. It's your life. You ain't gotta try to impress nobody. Remember that," he said before extending his hand to me.

"I appreciate it," I said, shaking his hand.

"You know I'm happy to hear that you don't talk like them lil ignorant bastards passing themselves off as teenagers these days. 'Yaknowwhati'msayingshawtyfolk.' I'm like 'no, what are you saying? and I ain't short. I'm six feet three inches tall.' I'm glad you can talk like you got some sense in your head."

"Thanks, my man. You take care," I said with a chuckle.

I got off the bus right in front of the Art Institute of Atlanta and ran across East Ponce de Leon to a tall high-rise building where Kwame's lawyer had her office. I walked into the building and headed over to the information desk in the center of the lobby. I asked the receptionist to ring the lawyer's phone, but before she could punch in a number, I saw the tall, well-dressed black woman rushing past me.

"Hey! Mrs. Ross," I called out.

Yolanda Ross exemplified class and poise. I don't know where my brother found her, but I was glad he did. She looked to be in her early thirties, but the most striking thing about her was how beautiful she could be without any hair on her head. She stopped and turned my way. She smiled at me with those perfectly white teeth.

"Hey, Romeo. How are you doing?" she said.

"Am I late?"

"Late for what?" she asked with a frown on her face.

"I thought we had a meeting today."

"No. But I'm meeting with your brother today. As a matter of fact, that's where I'm headed now."

"What's going on?"

"The parole hearing is today," she said, moving steadily toward the door. "Did you forget?"

"I thought that was tomorrow. I guess I got everything mixed up."

"It's okay. You're more than welcome to ride with me if you like, but we have to leave right now," she said, tapping a diamond-studded watch.

My heart started racing. I hustled over and followed her out the big glass doors. A driver held the door of a Lincoln Town Car, and I climbed in the backseat after her. The driver closed the door and we were off to the Atlanta Federal Penitentiary.

"So what do you think is gonna happen?" I asked the minute we were in our seat belts.

"Hard to say. Things can be a little unpredictable at these parole hearings. Sometimes it seems that the state is more interested in keeping bodies in the cages than actually rehabilitating them."

"What do you mean?"

"Prisons are big businesses, Romeo. The inmates work all day for twelve cents an hour. That's not even a fraction of minimum wage. So if a company wants to make a big profit on its product, they go to the prisons so they can cut down on their labor cost. Why do you think they are building prisons right and left and won't invest one brick in a new college? Let that be a lesson to you. Trouble is easy to find and hard to get out of. And the reason it's hard to get out of is because your body is a valuable asset to the government."

My heart stopped racing and fell out on the floor.

"In other words, you don't think my brother is coming home."

"I didn't say that, but I don't want you to get your hopes up too high. Parole is a tough task, especially on the first go-round. But let's stay positive and prayerful," she said as she opened her briefcase and removed some papers. "I have some other things in line for Kwame if this doesn't work out. His appeal is still in the works."

The winds were taken from beneath my sails, and I was quiet for the rest of the trip. Mrs. Ross tapped my leg and mouthed the words *don't worry* before she stuck her cell phone up to her ear and chatted away with someone at the prison. I turned and stared out the window, closing my eyes and saying a silent prayer for my brother's return.

4

ROMEO

We made it to the massive structure that was the Atlanta Federal Penitentiary. To me, the building itself
was a crime deterrent. Fear kicked into overdrive as we
passed through fence after fence topped off with con-
certina wire. Guard towers were everywhere, and straight-
faced men with rifles paced back and forth, looking for
signs of trouble from a place that housed some of the
world's most dangerous criminals. I hated that my brother
was among them.

As we made our way onto the grounds, I saw a sea of
black faces in the recreation yard on the side of the prison.
The driver opened the car door and two guards escorted
us inside.

We were searched, pushed through a metal detector,
then quickly ushered down a long corridor. I don't know
why but I was petrified. Ever since I could remember, I've
been deathly afraid of prisons. I had visited Kwame only
once since he had been incarcerated, because I couldn't

shake the nightmares of the first time I visited him. We passed an inmate who was mopping the floor. He looked to be in his late twenties. He stopped what he was doing and openly lusted after me as if I were some pretty girl. I frowned and kept walking. I was quite offended but I wasn't about to get into it with a sexually confused convict. He made a kissing sound and I turned around. He held up his hand and motioned for me to come to him. I gave him the finger and walked into the meeting room with Mrs. Ross and the guard.

The room was a plain and dull white with a long table and a few chairs. There were no windows or pictures on the wall, just a big square room. Mrs. Ross pointed to a chair in the corner, and I took a seat. A few minutes later, people started entering the room and taking their seats at the long table. My eyes lit up when Kwame was escorted into the room by a Hulk-looking correction officer. The officer nodded at him and gave him a thumbs-up. Kwame wore a matching khaki shirt and pants with a prison number stenciled across the left breast pocket. We both shared the same dark chocolate complexion, but he was taller and seemed to have muscles bulging from everywhere. We made eye contact, and he tossed his head back to say "what's up" before taking his seat. The parole panel was made up of one woman and two men.

"Thank you for coming," said the white woman, who looked to be old enough to have eaten at the Last Supper, before introducing the panel.

"Now, Mr. Kwame Braxton, why should we release you back into society?" the same white lady said.

"Well"—Kwame cleared his throat—"I know saying this may not help my cause, but I never should've been here in the first place. But since I've been here, I've kept my nose clean, and I've done almost a year's worth of college correspondence courses."

"It says here that you were placed in disciplinary dorms twice during your incarceration. Care to explain?" the woman asked.

"Ma'am, with all due respect, it's almost impossible to do two years in prison without a few infractions. This is a very violent environment, and every day it gets worse. Gang activity is peeking at you around every corner, and sometimes asking them to leave you alone just isn't enough. It's not like in the streets where if someone bumps into you, you can say excuse me and walk on. In here if someone bumps you and you try to walk away, they're going to think they can take advantage of you. So sometimes you have to fight just to keep the peace, not to mention your manhood. I'm not making excuses; it's just the way it is in here."

"Based on the severity of your crimes and the total lack of remorse on your part," said a white man, who looked to be about Kwame's age, "I'm finding it hard to vote that you be paroled."

"Sir, I can't be remorseful for something I didn't do. You guys want me to—"

Mrs. Ross drummed her fingers on the table and Kwame stopped talking.

"You were convicted by a jury of your peers. And for the sake of argument, let's say you are innocent. Then why would you sign a plea agreement basically admitting to the crime you claim you didn't commit?"

"I took the plea because seven years, with the possibility of parole after two, was better than twenty-five. Contrary to your guys' opinion, I'm not some drug lord who can afford the dream team to prove my innocence."

"The court assigned you an attorney."

"Is that what you call him? He might as well have been called a public pretender. Look, I'm not trying to sound cynical or anything, but that guy was incompetent, and if you do a little research, you'll see that since my case, he's been disbarred and is working as a stockbroker or something. Going to law school was something he did to appease his parents. If I would've taken his advice, I would've gotten the electric chair. So seeing what I was dealing with, I just took the deal."

"I see that you have the same attitude you had at your trial. Nothing is your fault," the young white guy said.

Kwame started to say something but caught himself. He took a deep breath and exhaled.

"You don't have anything to say for yourself?" the same guy asked.

"All I have to say is this system is not perfect. I was seventeen years old when I came in here. I was headed off to my freshman year at the University of South Carolina. For the life of me, I can't understand why you guys are so hell bent on ruining my life."

"Try looking in the mirror at the person who is ruining your life. We didn't put crack cocaine in your possession. We didn't put two pounds of marijuana in your possession. That was all you," the other guy on the panel—a black guy—said.

Kwame sighed and shook his head. "All I'm saying is if you guys believe that everyone behind these walls is guilty and not one of them has been wrongfully convicted, then I guess I won't make parole."

When Kwame said that, I felt as if my heart were going to fall out of my chest. I wished he would just shut up, or if he insisted on talking, just tell the people what they wanted to hear so we could get out of here.

"The system is not the issue here. We're talking about you. I'll tell you right now that your attitude is not helping your cause at all," the old white lady said as if she were reading my mind.

"I've done two years in prison for a crime I didn't commit. I'm nineteen years old, and all I really want to do is get on with my life. Now, being that you guys are trying to keep me in here has me a little upset, but I understand."

"You understand what?" the white guy asked.

"What I'm dealing with."

"Care to elaborate?" the black guy said.

"Guilty or not, this is my first offense. Before this, I never had so much as a traffic ticket, so at the very least, I would be considered a nonviolent offender, yet I'm in here with some of the worst people you could ever imagine. Murderers, rapists, child molesters—people who will never see the streets again as free men. People who will try to sabotage any possibility of release just for the sake of being evil. So, yes, there were times when I had to stand up for myself, but if you read the reports, you'll see that I was never the aggressor."

"Have you ever seen a crack baby?" the black man asked.

I wanted to scream, "I'm looking at one," but I knew Kwame and Mrs. Ross would've slapped me silly, so I kept my comments to myself.

"Excuse me?" Kwame asked.

"Have you ever seen a crack baby?" he barked, slamming his hand down on the table.

"I'm sure I have," Kwame answered quietly.

"Do you realize people like you contribute to that?"

"Sir, that crack was not mine. The car wasn't mine. I was doing a favor for a friend"—Kwame started, but was cut off.

"Yeah, yeah, yeah. We've all heard your story and the jury didn't buy it and I'm sure this board isn't buying it either. Now"—he rustled through some papers—"you were sentenced to seven years, and you could be, and I stress *could be,* paroled after two years."

Kwame looked over to Mrs. Ross, who nodded that everything was okay.

"But I'm not sure you are rehabilitated," he said.

"Sir, I'm very familiar with drug addicts. I'm not proud of some of the choices I've made. Some of the people I chose to hang around. Being in here has given me time to see the things I could've done differently to change my situation," Kwame said.

"What are your plans *if*—and trust me, it's a big 'if'— we were to grant you parole?" the white guy asked.

"I plan to get a job. I plan to be the best role model I can be for my brother. I plan to be the man my grandmother raised me to be."

"There's something about you that makes me believe you're a con artist who's still trying to get over. I think the minute you see the light of freedom, you will be back to selling drugs," the black man said with a self-righteous look on his face.

"I can't go back to selling drugs because I never sold them in the first place," Kwame said.

"You're in prison for it," the black man snapped, sitting back in his chair and crossing his arms with a smug look on his face.

"What's wrong with you?" I screamed, surprising myself with my outburst. I couldn't sit there quietly anymore.

"Romeo," Kwame said, shaking his head. He was pleading with his eyes for me to sit down, but my blood had risen to its highest level, and I was about to blow a vessel.

"No," I snapped. "I wanna know why this man is trying to keep you locked up. You're acting like he murdered somebody. You just want to keep him locked up so you can make some money off of him. He's not a slave. He did time in your dumb little prison, now leave him alone!" I yelled.

"Remove him from the hearings," the black man shouted, pointing his finger at the door. "I'm so sick of these ghetto bastards that I don't know what to do. If you ask me, we should do our race a favor and exterminate every last one of the little ignorant—" he said before catching himself.

Mrs. Ross stood and stormed toward me. She grabbed my arm and snatched me up like I was an unruly toddler.

"What was that?" she asked once we were in the hallway.

"Did you hear what he said?" My eyes were wide with disbelief.

"What was that?" she snapped again.

"I just couldn't sit there and listen to that man treat my brother like that."

"I want you to calm down. That little charade did not help your brother's cause at all. That's what they do. It's all a game to try to provoke him. Kwame is doing fine."

"And why are you just sitting there? I thought you were his lawyer. You're not saying anything."

"Romeo, Kwame is in jail. That means he's the property of the state. This is not a television show. This is real, and until you take a few classes in criminal law, I suggest you keep your comments to yourself."

Reality hit me and I felt like a complete idiot. I leaned on the wall and slid down to the floor.

God, I hope I didn't ruin his chances, I thought.

Mrs. Ross walked over and leaned down to squeeze my shoulder. "Just relax. I know this is very difficult, but we have to stay the course and play by the rules. Okay?"

I nodded my head.

Mrs. Ross walked back toward the room. She paused and gave me a reassuring smile before she entered the room.

I tried to calm myself by standing up and taking a walk. Then I sat down. But I couldn't sit still, so I stood again and paced the halls. I sat back down and got up again. It seemed like they were taking forever in there. I prayed that I hadn't hurt Kwame's chances of coming home, but something inside of me told me that I had done just that. How would he ever forgive me? I know *I* would never forgive myself. And what would Nana do? Oh, my God. How could I ever face Nana if I was the reason Kwame wasn't coming home? I sat back down and jumped right back up when that confused convict with the mop came walking my way. I looked around for a guard or somebody, but all I saw was a long, empty corridor. I started to go knock on the door, but I had already caused enough confusion today. But I would yell if he made a move toward me. And if that didn't work, I would bite him.

"What's your name, sexy?" he asked, lust oozing from his words. "You a pretty lil something."

"Man, I don't know what your problem is, but you need to leave me alone."

"No need for all the hostilities. I'm just making conversation," he said, steadily walking toward me, looking over his shoulder as he approached. I guess he was trying to make sure the coast was clear. "You're so damn cute."

This was crazy. The guy didn't look gay to me—at least not what I thought gay should look like, but this was a prison, so I guess anything went. He had more muscles than Kwame, a bald head, and a nasty scar going down his face. I imagined that scar came from him trying to hit on the wrong dude. Mr. Confused walked closer to me and looked me up and down before licking his lips. I stopped being scared and became disgusted. He walked past me and peeked into the door window of the room of the parole hearing. He did a double take and his whole demeanor changed. His eyes bulged as if he had just stepped on a land mine. His lust turned to nervousness.

"You here for Kwame?"

"That's my brother," I said, trying to capitalize on his sudden apprehension.

"Damn," he said with a nervous smile. "I was just playing with you earlier. You know that, right?"

"Whatever."

"Hey, you don't even bother telling your brother because he ain't gonna do nothing but act a fool. He's about to get out, so if I were you, I wouldn't tell him nothing. He ain't got no sense of humor," he said as all of his lustful bravado turned to fear. He looked back at the room where Kwame was before almost running down the hallway.

I thought about the look of sheer terror on Mr. Confused's face and wondered what kind of guy Kwame had become in this place.

Before I could finish my thought, Mrs. Ross walked out and motioned for me to follow her.

"What happened?" I said, following her. She didn't answer as we were escorted out of the building the same way we had come in.

"He's not getting out, is he?" I asked just as the fresh air entered my lungs.

She ignored me and kept walking until we were outside and standing by the car.

"Come on, Mrs. Ross. Tell me something," I pressed. My nerves were on edge, and I couldn't take the silent treatment.

The driver opened the door for her and she got in the car. I stood outside looking down at her.

"Are you planning to walk?" she asked with a hint of irritation on her face. I couldn't help but think that she had gotten some bad news.

"Why won't you answer me?"

"Romeo, get in this car before someone mistakes you for an inmate."

I huffed a bit but thought about all of the other guys who kept Mr. Confused company and got in the car.

"What happened to your hand?" she asked, and I buckled my seat belt.

"I hurt it jumping a fence," I answered reluctantly. "What's going on with my brother?"

"Is that injury going to stop you from playing football on Friday?"

"No," I snapped. "Who cares anyway? I wanna know about my brother."

"Calm down. I'm only asking because I would hate for Kwame to come see your game and have you not be able to throw one of those touchdown passes you like to brag about."

I stared at the lawyer. What she said didn't register until she flashed the prettiest smile I had ever seen.

"He has to sign some papers, but he should be home in time to make your game Friday night," she said, shaking her head.

"Are you serious?" I asked.

"As a heart attack."

"Yeah!" I yelled, pumping my fist. "That's what I'm talking about. If he had you in the beginning, he wouldn't have been in there in the first place. Man, I thought I messed up his chances."

"Actually, you helped. Your outburst exposed one of the board members as a racist. The only black man at that," she said, shaking her head. "After that, it was pretty obvious they had ulterior motives. I made a phone call to the deputy warden and told him what transpired, and, well, let's just say, he's going to make this right. Better let him go than to face a discrimination lawsuit."

I felt like jumping through the sunroof and yelling to God how awesome He was. So that's what I did.

5

ROMEO

Mrs. Ross had her driver stop in front of my building. I gave her a big hug and quickly jumped from the Lincoln. I couldn't get to Nana quick enough. I took off through the breezeway and almost tripped over General Mack, who was lying on the hard concrete, just as I turned the corner.

"You kicked me, boy?" he said, looking up at me with an ugly scowl on his scrubby face.

"Man, why you lying right there anyway? You gonna make somebody trip and fall," I said.

General Mack jumped to his feet with his back to me. He straightened his back and slapped his hands down on both thighs, saluted an imaginary person, then did an about-face, turning one hundred and eighty degrees so that he was facing me. He stumbled a little bit, caught himself, and relaxed his posture. He looked me up and down as if I was facing inspection.

"Who you think you talking to?" he snapped.

"Oh, Lord," I said.

"I see you got on your Easter shoes. Them some ugly slip and slides, boy. Where you coming from?"

"Went to see Kwame. He's coming home," I said with a wide smile.

"Okay, yeah. That's good news. We could always use a few more good soldiers in the battle."

"A'ight, General. I gotta get inside to tell Nana the good news."

"I'm the general and you just a corporal. So how you gonna excuse yourself when you haven't been properly dismissed?" he asked, snapping his posture back as straight as he could. "Ahhh Teeeen Tion!" he barked.

"General, I can't play your lil army game today. I gotta go," I said, walking past him.

"So you just gonna be disrespectful?" he said, looking as if he was genuinely hurt.

I stopped and dropped my head. I sighed my frustration but walked back to him and stood perfectly still.

A smile eased through his raggedy gray beard. "As you were, soldier."

I waited on the nut to tell me I could leave. *Boy, the things I do for my elders,* I thought as I stood there looking stupid.

"Before I dismiss you, got some news for you to carry on," he said.

"Come on, General," I said, squirming in place. "I gotta go."

"Stand down, soldier," he barked as if he really had some control. "I said I got some news for you."

"What's the news, General?" I said, shaking my head at

myself for standing here and pacifying this full-fledged, shell-shocked alcoholic.

"Your mother's in trouble," he said, placing a folded envelope in the palm of my hand. "Do your due diligence."

"General, what are you talking about?"

"You're dismissed," he said, snapping his hand up into a salute and slapping his own face to the point where even he frowned. "Damn." He grimaced. He put his hand back down and turned on his heels, tripping before marching off to his own little la-la land.

I slipped the piece of paper in my pocket and went into my apartment.

"Nana," I called out.

No answer.

I walked to her bedroom and eased the door open. She was sleeping soundly. I decided to let her get her rest. Maybe I would let Kwame's homecoming be a surprise. I eased the door closed and went into my room to get out of those tight shoes and slick pants. I quickly changed into the sweat suit that I would wear to football practice. I grabbed the envelope that General Mack had given me. I opened it up and saw there was nothing inside. The outside was only addressed to "The Residents of 245 Harrington Way, Atlanta, GA, 30031." I tossed it on my dresser and left the apartment.

I looked around for General Mack to see if he could tell me why he gave me an empty envelope, but he was nowhere to be found. I walked over to Amir's place to pick him up for practice, and when I knocked on the door, his eight-year-old sister, Malaya, opened it.

"Heeey, cutie pie," I said, reaching down and pinching her chubby cheek.

"Hey, Romeo," she said before running back to her television show.

"You doing good in school?" I asked Malaya.

"Nope," Miss Jackson, Amir and Malaya's mom, said, wheeling herself into the living room. "Bad as she can be."

"That's not true, Romeo," Malaya said, rolling her eyes at her mother.

"Roll another eye and I'll knock you into next week," Miss Jackson said, even though anybody with eyes knew it was an idle threat. She was paralyzed after being shot by a stray bullet from the gun of a ten-year-old wannabe gang member. Now she got around the neighborhood in a wheelchair that had seen better days.

Malaya rolled her eyes again, then went back to watching television.

"How you doing today, Miss Jackson?" I asked. "Outside of looking for a fight."

"Fight?" she said, looking around the apartment. "Ain't nobody round here can beat me."

"Well, how are you doing?" I asked again.

"Boy, if I was doing any better, I'd be sitting on His lap."

"On whose lap?"

"God's lap, fool. Who you think I'm talking about?"

"I don't know. I thought you might've been talking about some little man you were getting your creep on with round here."

"Shut yo mouth." She blushed. "You know I had a dream about fish last night, and who is the first person I see in my house? You! So who you got pregnant?"

"Miss Jackson, why you always trying me? Maybe Amir got somebody pregnant. Why it gotta be me?"

"Boy, you know Amir ain't gonna bust a grape with

Welch's permission," she said, laughing at her own joke. "It's you. Sure as I'm sitting here."

"Wrong. I'm a virgin," I said, smiling as I walked into Amir's room.

"Yeah, right," Miss Jackson said to my back. "And Denzel Washington is my baby daddy."

Amir's room was a hot mess. He called it "the head-quarters," but it looked like someone's hindquarters. One wall was painted black, one was bloodred, one was dark green, and the other one was the ugliest yellow I had ever seen in my life. The walls were adorned with posters of his heroes. Huey P. Newton, of the Black Panthers, was sitting in a straw wingback chair holding two rifles. H. Rap Brown pointed an accusing finger at somebody, and Malcolm X peeked out of a window while holding an AK-47 assault rifle. Martin Luther King frowned as he delivered his "I Have a Dream" speech.

The stereo was blasting something from Public Enemy.

"I got so much trouble on my mind," Public Enemy's Chuck D shouted. "Refuse to lose."

Amir didn't even hear me enter his room. He sat at his desk in front of his computer, bobbing his head up and down as his favorite rapper of all time told the white power structure to kiss him where the sun didn't shine.

"Don't move!" I yelled, sticking my finger in his neck.

He jumped and turned around, scared out of his mind.

"Got dog it, Romeo! Don't be coming in here with all that foolishness. This is a place of business," Amir said, hitting the STOP button on the CD player.

"My bad. Don't want to mess up the struggle," I said, slapping him on the back.

"While you playing"—Amir reached over and pulled a

paper off the printer and handed it to me—"check this out."

"What's this?" I said, looking at a letter addressed to the governor of Georgia.

"I'm trying to get a new law passed that says liquor stores in the hood can't open up until after five o'clock in the afternoon. I'm sending one to the mayor too."

I started laughing and he snatched the paper back.

"Think about it, Romeo. Why they gotta open before five? See, if we get this law passed, then we'll get rid of half the bums in the hood. If a brother gotta wait until five o'clock before he can get his drink on, then he might as well get a job. He should be working anyway."

"I hear ya. Where do I sign?"

"That's a good idea."

"What?"

"A petition." Amir pulled out a blank piece of paper.

"Good luck," I said, signing my name on the blank sheet.

"I don't know why we gotta have a liquor store on every other corner anyway. I'm about to try to get another law passed that says two liquor stores cannot be within a twenty-mile radius of an already-standing liquor store."

"Man, get ready for practice. You have the rest of your life to save the hood."

"That's where ya wrong, black man. Time is ticking and we're about to be extinct."

"Guess what?" I said.

"What?" Amir snapped.

"I was on the bus today going to see Kwame, and I met a fan of yours. He was talking about how good you were."

"For real?" Amir's eyes grew wide.

"Said he was gonna go out and try to find a jersey with your number on it. What is your number anyway, Amir?"

Amir narrowed his eyes. Realizing that I was playing him, he stuck his middle finger up at me. He got up and pulled his sports bag out of the closet.

"Come on, fool. I'm only on that old stinking team because you begged me to play. I don't give a rat's butt about no football, and you got the nerve to have jokes," he said, walking out of the room. "Bye, Mom. I'll see you after practice."

"Amir, you got some money?" Malaya asked.

"Nope."

"Man," she pouted. "I'm hungry."

Amir looked at me. I pulled out a ten-dollar bill and handed it to him.

"I'll give it back to you this weekend when we get paid."

We worked part-time at North DeKalb Mall in the Foot Locker sports store. Not only did it put a little extra change in our pockets, but more important, it also kept us rocking those fire tennis shoes the minute they hit the shelves.

"It's all good," I said, happy I could help out my best boy.

"Get Mommy something too," he said, handing his little sister the money. "We out."

"Romeo, you better start saving your money. You sho nuff got a baby on the way," Miss Jackson said.

"Thanks for telling me, and while you're rolling around the house all day, why don't you start your own psychic hotline?" I said, closing the door behind me.

"I just might do that," she said through the door.

6

ROMEO

Practice was brutal. The team did so many up/downs that even I felt sorry for them. I sat on the sideline talking to my position coach about what we did wrong in last week's game. I had to admit that I did get the royalty treatment and was never the target of any of my coaches' wrath. When practice was over, I made my way over to the bleachers and took a seat. Amir walked over to me.

"Man, I think Coach done lost his mind," he said. You couldn't find a clean spot on his body. He looked like he had just gotten back from taking a walk through a muddy valley. His eyes ran up and down my body. Noticing I was clean as the board of health, he frowned. "Why you so clean?"

"Quarterback's meeting," I said with a smile. "Sorry about that, bro."

"Aww, you must be crazy. I'm about to quit."

"You promise?" Coach Planter, our head football coach, said, walking up and slapping Amir on the back. "Amir, you don't know how bad I've been praying that I would one day hear those words come outta your mouth."

"Coach. You know we can't win without me," Amir said.

"I'm beginning to think we can't win *with* you," Coach said before turning to me. "Romeo, I got a stack of mail for you in my office. Make sure you come by there and get it. You decided on a school yet?"

"Nope."

"Florida State's been knocking pretty hard," he said, pumping up his alma mater.

"Tell 'em to keep on knocking," Amir said. "I'm his agent and whoever wants his services will need to come through me."

"Amir," Coach said in a soft tone. "Shut up."

"Ask Romeo if you don't believe me," Amir said. "We going to school together, and if I don't approve, then it ain't happening. So you tell your lil raggedy alma mater that we ain't going down to no Tallahassee."

"You wanna run a few more laps around the field?" Coach asked.

"That would be a resounding no, sir."

"Well, hush," Coach said.

Amir placed a hand over his mouth. Coach Planter shook his head and laughed. "You know I'm going to miss you, Amir. You are truly one of a kind."

"I'm going to miss you too, Coach. You are like three or four of a kind, but I wouldn't trade you for a box of rocks," Amir said, taking a jab at how fat our coach was.

"I'll be there in a minute, Coach," I said.

"Okay," he said before jokingly lunging at Amir, causing him to jump back into a fighter's stance. "Don't get jacked up, lil boy."

"Coach, this ain't what you want. Hey, you got any letters for me?" Amir asked.

"Yeah, a bunch of hate mail," Coach Planter said over his shoulder.

"Coach always tryna Jones somebody with his fat butt. Talking about he was a running back in college. Must've been running back and forth to the cafeteria," Amir said. "Gonna send me to Wendy's for his lunch today. Talking about he's watching his weight. That fool ordered a chicken salad, two biggie fries, two large Frostys, and an apple pie. I'm like, what does this fool eat when he ain't watching his weight? A whole cow?"

"You know, if your political career doesn't work out, you can always be a comedian," I said, laughing.

"Wrong! Didn't I tell you that's what's wrong with black people in the first place? We got too many corny comedians already. I'm a revolutionary, not some clown." He pointed toward our coach, who was wobbling his way into the building. "You ever wonder how he fits that wide load on a toilet seat? I bet he goes through three or four of those things a month."

"You got problems, bro," I said. "You have some serious problems."

"Looka here, looka here. If it ain't Cinderella," Amir said, turning his attention to a black two-seater Mercedes-Benz speeding its way into the athletic-field parking lot.

I met her when I was eight years old. The only boy in the entire projects who had to take piano lessons. I hated my grandmother for making me go to those stupid classes. All of my friends were playing summer league basketball, and there I was sitting in a hot room with an old choir director who smelled like Vicks VapoRub.

That was, until Ngiai showed up. She was the prettiest thing I had ever seen. She was a year younger than me but was already a four-year veteran of the ivories and in my same grade. We struck up a fast friendship, and we've never parted ways since that day.

Amir ran over to the car. I got up and slowly trudged my way over to where she had stopped.

"I got the front seat," Amir said, pulling at the door.

"Amir, if you don't go somewhere and wash your nasty butt . . . ," Ngiai snapped as she hit the power locks before Amir could open the door.

"Look at her, Rome. Living out in Fayetteville done made her bougie. She ain't act like that when she was slumming with us over in the hood."

"Shut up, boy," Ngiai said, putting her car in park and opening the sunroof.

"Hey, you," I said, leaning in for a kiss, but she recoiled as if I were a snake. She did offer her cheek, though.

"Ain't that cute," Amir said, shaking his head. "You know what? Forget all of that. Y'all been together too long. It's time for y'all to experience new people. Ngiai, from this day on, you gonna be my woman, which gives me the right to knock the taste outta you if you so much as desire to get a jazzy lip. And, Romeo, you can go date one of your groupies. Now that's final."

"Why are you so dirty?" Ngiai said, ignoring Amir's comments as she always did.

"Because"—Amir looked down at himself and smiled—"unlike the chosen one here, I had to practice. Some of us have to work for a living. I come out here to work, not to sit around like some prima donna looking at clipboards all day."

"Well, it's not like you couldn't use the practice, Amir. Do you know how to catch? You could've had three interceptions Friday night, and we might've won the game, but, noooo, you gotta suck up the place. And then you had the nerve to start dancing the one time you did do something. You are pitiful."

"Ngiai, don't you dare start with me. All them free throws you been missing. Clank. I'ma start calling you 'brick city.' Who in the heck wears mascara on the basketball court? Who you think you is?"

"Awww. Come here and give me a hug," Ngiai said, walking over to Amir with her arms outstretched. "It's not your fault."

"What's not my fault?" Amir asked, confused.

"You're retarded and nobody ever told you," Ngiai said with a sad face.

"Get off me, girl. You retarded," Amir said, slapping her hand down and swelling up like he was ready to fight.

"You better get your little dwarf butt out of my face," she snapped, not backing down.

"Who you calling a dwarf? I bet you won't be calling me a dwarf when I pick you up and body slam your skinny lil butt down on this asphalt. You know I'll fight a girl."

"And I'll fight a midget. Move out of my way, lil boy."

"Make me, skinny girl."

Ngiai pushed Amir and he stumbled back about ten steps, flailing his arms and trying desperately not to fall down. He finally found his balance.

"Dag, girl, you strong. You sure you ain't a man?" Amir said, walking over to Ngiai and acting as if he was going to pull her pants down. "Let me check out your anatomy."

"Your mother's a man," Ngiai snapped, slapping his hand away from her. "Get your filthy hands off of me."

"Hey, don't be talking about my momma," Amir said as if he was really offended. "I'm serious. I done beat folks down for less than that."

"Get outta my face, Amir."

"Make me."

I watched the two of them go back and forth like I was at a tennis match. My two favorite friends in the world had a love-hate relationship with each other, and it had been that way since the day they met.

Ngiai was five foot nine, and she had to look down at Amir, but he was holding his own before Ngiai hauled off and slapped him hard across his face.

"Ouch." Amir turned to me, holding his head. "You better get your girl, Romeo, before I break my foot off in her lil narrow butt. I don't play nobody putting they hands on me or talking about my momma, and she done broke both of the rules."

I threw my hands up to let him know that I wasn't in it.

"I'ma go grab a quick shower. Get myself fresh to death like I do, and when I come back, you better be sitting here waiting on me with that lil raggedy car at the temperature that I like. You got that, broad?" Amir said with his finger pointed at Ngiai.

"I didn't bring my booster seat, and I'm not getting a ticket messing around with you," Ngiai said just before she slapped his hand down.

Amir flinched at her and she reached out and slapped him again. He grabbed his face and shook his head as if he was forcing himself not to go after her. He stuck up his middle finger and walked off toward the showers.

"Do y'all have to argue all the time?" I asked.

"I'm not thinking about Amir with his half-grown self."

"Why are you still up here?" I asked. "I thought y'all practiced right after school?"

"We do. I came to see you," she said, her expression turning serious.

"I'm surprised Coach Reeder doesn't have you in there still shooting free throws."

"Man, don't even mention those words. I know I shot a thousand of those things today. By the time I finished, I could barely lift my arms."

"I bet you won't miss anymore when the game is on the line."

"Who are you telling?" Ngiai lifted her arm and grimaced. "I won't miss anymore, period."

She walked over and sat on the trunk of her car. Her mood changed again. She sighed, then looked away. Something was bothering her. I knew her in and out. I could read her like a book, and those hazel eyes always told me her deepest secrets.

"What's going on?" I asked.

She looked at me, then turned away again. I knew her better than she knew herself, so I sat down beside her and gave her a minute to find the words.

"Romeo, we will always be friends," she said, shaking her head. A tear welled in her eye.

"What are you talking about?"

"I think our relationship has run its course."

"Run its course? What are you talking about? Where is all this coming from?"

"I can't give you what you want. Not right now."

"And what is it that you think I want, Ngiai?"

She sighed and wiped her eyes. "I know what's going on. I'm not stupid, Romeo," she said.

"What are you talking about?"

"I'm talking about Vonetta and how she's running around here telling any and everybody that she's having your baby."

My baby!

"You gotta be kidding me!" I snapped.

"Do I look like I'm kidding?"

The tears streaming down her mocha-colored cheeks said that this was far from a joke.

"Man, Vonetta's lying. I never touched that girl," I said.

"Romeo, stop. Just stop. I see her up in your face all the time."

"And guys are up in your face too. Does that mean you're sexing 'em up?" I replied.

"No, it doesn't, but I'm not the one running around here like a horny little toad all the time. Besides, the guys I talk to are strictly friends, and you know that."

"No, I don't know that. I trust what you tell me. But whatever. Why you gotta go there?"

"Listen," she said, throwing her hands up, surrendering before this conversation turned into an argument. "I know you wanna have sex. I know you believe that you need to have sex, and I'm not ready to go there. So, hey, I understand. Do you. And from this point on, you don't have to worry about me standing in your way."

"Ngiai, save it. It's not that deep."

"Obviously it is. So what should I do? Sit around looking dumb and twiddling my thumbs until she has the baby? And then what? Sit around and play stepmom? I'm not that desperate. Why would she lie anyway?"

"Why does anybody lie? The need for attention, low self-esteem, jealousy. Maybe her daddy didn't hug her enough. I don't know."

"Ahh," she growled before standing up. "This is too much. Every week it's a different story about a different girl. Look, if sex is that important to you, then you can go out there and sow your little oats to your heart's content, but I'm not going there."

"You know what? If you're that weak, then maybe I should go holla at somebody else. I already told you it wasn't that serious, but you're not hearing me."

"Right. I'm not hearing you because you're full of it. Every time we're alone together, you're humping all over me like some dog in heat. You know it's not going anywhere, but I guess you think you're going to get me excited enough to go there. Instead of respecting my wishes, you try to manipulate the situation as if I can't resist you. But the thing is, if you know I really don't want to go there, then why can't you respect that? Anyway, all of that is irrelevant now."

"Okay, I'm attracted to my girlfriend. Sue me."

"Don't try to play me, Romeo," she said, looking directly into my eyes. "Do I look stupid to you?"

"No, but you're wrong on this one," I said.

"According to Vonetta, I'm right."

"Man, forget Vonetta. And since when did you start believing Vonetta over me? She's lying."

Ngiai stood up and walked around to the driver's side and snatched open the door. She reached into the backseat and fumbled around with something before coming out with a picture. In the picture, I was lying on a bed shirtless, with my arms behind my head and Vonetta lying on my chest. The only thing she was wearing was a thong and a smile. I stood staring at the picture with my lip hanging down to the ground.

I looked up and saw a broken and defeated look on Ngiai's face. Tears were flowing from those oceans she used to navigate her way through this world. I was still in shock and didn't know what to say. She turned away from me, and all I could do was wish I could take back what I had done.

Ngiai took a deep breath and brushed past me. She got into her car and gave me one last look. I tried to move, but my feet were stuck to the asphalt. Seeing my girl hurt like that over my stupidity made me feel even worse.

"Wait a minute," I finally got out, but it was too late. The little car was speeding away. I watched as the tiny red taillights zigzagged out of the parking lot, and I couldn't help but feel the love of my life slipping away. My stomach was in knots as I looked to the heavens for answers that I knew wouldn't rain down on me.

Amir walked out of the locker room and came over to me. I was standing in the same spot, still staring at the last place I had seen Ngiai's car. He saw the look on my face and turned to see that Ngiai was gone.

"What you do?" he said.

"I think your mother may be a psychic for real."

7

ROMEO

Rinnnnnnng! Rinnnnnnnng! Rinnnnnnnng! I rolled over and hit the alarm.

Rinnnnnnnng!

"What the . . . ," I said, fumbling around to pick up my cell phone. "Hello," I said, sleep still calling my name.

"What you doing?" a sassy voice said on the other end of the line.

I looked at the clock. It was five-thirty in the morning, and I still had another hour before I had to rise and shine.

"Who is this?"

"This is the love of your life, Vonetta."

"Whatchu want?" I said to the root of all that was evil in my life.

"I heard I got you in a little trouble," she said with a little chuckle. "My bad. My bad."

"So you think that's funny?" I said, sitting up on the side of the bed.

"Nah, man. I'm tryna figure out what's going on. Maybe I can help."

"What's up with that picture?"

"What picture?"

"Don't play stupid, Vonetta."

"Oh, that picture. Y'all broke up over that?"

"You doctored the thing up. Why you do that?"

"It's for my senior book," she said casually, as if her deeds hadn't ruined my life. "I thought I told you that."

"Yeah, but you didn't tell me you were gonna switch things around and make it look like we just finished doing cuttin'."

"But we did have sex. Just not that time."

"Girl, you so foul I can smell you all the way over here."

"Romeo, you don't love me?" she said with a laugh. "You know I love myself some Romeo."

"Man, stop playing so much. You need to leave that weed alone. You ain't my woman—Ngiai is."

"Boy, stop. Ngiai don't give you what you want 'cause she's too busy playing Goody Two-shoes. That's what you get for dealing with a bougie broad. You need a real chick like me in your life. Somebody who keeps it real. One hundred percent, all the time."

"Whatever. And what's this about you claiming you're pregnant by me?"

"Now, that part might be true."

I couldn't believe what I was hearing.

"Wait a minute. How you figure that?" I asked with my heart racing a million beats per second.

"Last I checked, Romeo, you was in advanced classes, so I know you know how people get pregnant."

"Have you been smoking?"

"Nope. Gotta make sure the baby don't come into this world addicted to the bud, so I'ma chill for a minute."

"Something has you trippin'. What are you talking about? If you pregnant, it's not mine."

"How do you know that?"

"Because it doesn't take being in advanced classes to know that condoms stop that kind of thing from happening. And being that you are one of those low-down skanks," I said, feeling myself getting angrier and angrier by the second, "I looked at it, made sure it didn't break; then I flushed it down the toilet. So save your crap for someone else."

"Did you know that about a million sperm cells can fit on the head of a needle?" Vonetta asked calmly, as if I weren't trying to bite her head off over the phone. "A million of those little rascals! And all it takes is one to do the job. Fertilize that egg and the next thing you know, we got us a lil Romeo running around here. And not the one from the TV show."

"Girl, you need to stop playing so much. And you better stop running around telling lies on me."

"I'm not lying," she spat.

"Well, what do you call it?"

"I missed my cycle, and the last dude I was with was you. If my memory serves me right, we did a whole lot before you went and got that condom, Romeo."

"You tryna trap me," I said calmly. "You think I'ma be your meal ticket? Well, you got another think coming. If you are pregnant, it's not mine. Get over yourself and go find another victim."

"Romeo, the world if full of high school big shots who work at McDonald's. Far as I'm concerned, you could be one of them. You ain't no LeBron James, so cut the crap. Ain't nobody tryna trap you."

"Whatever," I said, feeling a little dressed down by her dismissal. "You need to stop all that lying. I don't care what happens between me and Ngiai—you won't ever be my woman."

"If I have this baby, I'm going to be more than your woman, so I guess we'll see. Take care, sperm donor," she said before hanging up in my face.

Just as I was reaching over to put my cell phone back on the nightstand, I looked up and into Nana's eyes.

"I know I didn't raise the kind of young man I just heard on that telephone," she said with her hands on her hips and a frown on her face.

"Nana, that girl is lying on me. She's running round here telling everybody—"

"Shut up. I don't care what she's doing. You just shut your mouth right now. Now, did you have sex with that girl?"

"No."

"Okay, if I hear one more lie, I'ma walk over there and knock your teeth down the back of your lying throat."

Ouch!

"Now, I just heard you say something about a condom not breaking. What were you doing, playing water balloons with it?"

I looked down. Busted!

"Romeo, I raised you the best I knew how. I couldn't talk to you about the birds and the bees, but I always told you to be respectful to women. Didn't I?"

"Yes, ma'am. But that girl ain't."

"Ain't what? She was good enough for you to run

around here with and put your little pecker someplace where it wasn't supposed to be."

"But, Nana—" I started.

"Shut your mouth, boy. Lord knows I'm so disappointed in you. Now, I want you to get up and walk over to that mirror. Get up," she snapped.

I did as I was told. I stood in front of the mirror and took in my own reflection.

"You just stand there. Take some time to look at yourself and decide the kind of man you want to be. Do you wanna be a coward who runs away from his responsibility? Or do you want to be a man who stands up to it? If this young lady was good enough for you to share your body with, then she deserves to be treated with some respect. Now, if she's lying about this child, then that's her issue, but you . . . you will carry yourself with some dignity and respect. Sex is not a game. It's serious business, and that's why the good Lord said it was for married people. But you wanna be fast and just ignore the word of God. Now look what that got you. You just sinned your little butt into adulthood," she said, walking out of the room.

"Yes, ma'am," I said. Now I felt worse than I did before.

I rubbed my temples in an attempt to relieve some stress and took one last glance in the mirror. I balled up my fist and threw an air punch at myself.

"Nana," I called out, but all I got was a slammed door in response.

8

ROMEO

The school was all abuzz about Vonetta's so-called pregnancy. It seemed everywhere I turned, someone was gossiping about Vonetta or me. I scanned the commons area and found Vonetta standing with about three or four of her loud and ghetto fabulous girlfriends. One of the girls standing with her had blue hair, the other one had red hair, and I think I saw a shade of yellow in Vonetta's.

They are a hot mess. What was I thinking? I thought.

Vonetta seemed to be basking in all of the attention. Ngiai walked in and they all started laughing.

Ngiai turned around and said something, but I couldn't make it out. I waited to see if any type of drama was going to transpire, but Ngiai walked off. I shook my head and headed down the senior hallway. I was getting a book out of my locker when Vonetta walked up.

"You mad at me?" she said as she rubbed up close to me.

It seemed as if the entire student body stopped moving

and focused all of their attention on the two of us. I removed my book, closed my locker, and walked away without saying a word. I wasn't about to give her the satisfaction. I said what I had to say on the phone.

I walked the crowded halls of Tucker High School in a confused daze. Everyone who wasn't talking about the baby situation was talking about the big game Friday night. If we won, we would win the championship for the first time in the school's fifty-year history. And if I had to guess, I would say about ninety-nine percent of the student body told me I was the key to the school's victory. But for the first time since I had picked up the pigskin, football was the last thing on my mind.

"Good luck Friday night, Rome," I heard over and over as I roamed the halls. I always nodded my head and said thanks, but my mind just wasn't in it. I kept replaying the Vonetta situation over and over in my head and trying to see if we ever had any skin-to-skin contact. How unlucky could I be? My first time having sex, and I might end up being a father. On top of that, I was going to be stuck at the hip with Ms. Ghetto, which meant she was going to teach my child to be ghetto. I wanted to scream at the top of my lungs. If I had known it was going to turn out like this, I would've at least waited on Ngiai. At least I loved her. I couldn't stand Vonetta.

But something deep inside of me was telling me she was lying to everyone. But what if she was telling the truth? How was I going to go to college and still try to support a baby? Maybe college would have to wait. But then what kind of life was I going to have? Working as a day laborer or sweating in a plant wasn't what I had planned for my life.

"What's up, Rome?" one of my football teammates said. "How does it feel to be expecting?" He laughed and walked on.

I didn't respond.

"Romeo," a female friend said. "You slept with Vonetta? You are so gross," she said, making a gagging sound. "That girl is a garden tool."

"Romeo, if you need a babysitter for Friday, my lil sister said she'll hook you up," some clown I didn't even know said as he laughed a little too loud.

I ignored them all and walked to my class. My teacher, Mrs. Simpson, looked at me and shook her head. "I hope those are just rumors I'm hearing, Romeo," she said. She waited for an answer, but I didn't have anything to say. I just went to my seat.

"Everyone, settle down," Mrs. Simpson said as she turned to write the notes for today on the board.

"Excuse me, Mrs. Simpson," Carlos, the class clown, said. "Can we take up a collection for Romeo? You know he's gonna be a daddy, and we can't have the baby walking round here with a stinky booty."

"Go to hell, man," I snapped, jumping up from my chair and charging over to where Carlos was seated. "Say it again! Say anything else to me and I will knock your teeth out of your stupid mouth."

"Go on man." Carlos held up a hand to protect himself.

"That's what I thought, punk," I growled as I debated whether to take my frustrations out on his nappy head.

"Romeo," Mrs. Simpson yelled at me. "Out! Get out of my class and go straight to the office. And you tell Mr. Jacks that you cannot return to my class until you've learned to control your temper. I also want a written apology to everyone sitting in here. You understand?"

I walked back over to my desk, grabbed my book bag, and walked out of the class without answering her question. I walked down to the corridors to the office and realized for the first time in my life that I was in trouble in school. This Vonetta thing really had me riled up. Normally I was good at ignoring people. Growing up where I did, you had to have thick skin, but now I was starting to panic.

I walked into the front office and took a seat on the bench, where you could always find the school's troublemakers. I sat beside Willie, a short and stocky guy who had been in and out of juvenile detention centers since he was eight years old.

"Oh, Lord, the chosen one up in here," he said loud enough for the entire school to hear him. "What is this world coming to?"

"What's up, Willie?"

"Nothing much, playboy. Teachers round here tripping again. They won't let a brother get an education. I sneeze wrong and it's 'Go to the office, Willie,' " he said.

"What you do?"

"I ain't done nuttin'. Teachers are haters, player. The question is, whatchu do?"

I took a deep breath. "Cussed in class."

"What?" Willie exclaimed. "I cuss all the time. Every damn day. They best not say nuttin' to me 'bout no damn cussing. I'll cuss 'em all out. Ain't that right, madam secretary?"

I looked over at the secretary, who chuckled and shook her head.

"Boy, you're crazy," I said.

"What are you doing in here, Romeo?" the secretary asked me.

"Got kicked out of class," I said.

"Why?"

"Cussing."

"The use of profanity is a sign of a person with a limited vocabulary," she said, looking at Willie but talking to me. "I'll tell Mr. Jacks his star quarterback is out here waiting on him."

I nodded my head.

Willie fanned her off and stretched his legs out, flipped his body around until he was lying flat on the bench, then closed his eyes. Trouble was his friend, and he was definitely in his comfort zone.

I sat there for a little over thirty minutes, and while I waited, I started writing my letters of apology to my teacher and classmates. Just as I was finishing up letter number ten, I was summoned into Mr. Jacks's very spacious office.

"Have a seat, Romeo," Mr. Jacks said.

I had never been in the principal's office before. He was a thinly built man who stood a hair taller than Amir, so maybe he was five feet three inches tall. He had a mini-afro that was graying on the sides. I looked around the walls of his office and saw a slew of plaques and pictures covering the school's academic achievements over the years. Tucker had won the state championships in basketball, soccer, baseball, and football in previous years, yet there wasn't one single ribbon on the walls representing us. The word around school was that Mr. Jacks wasn't a big fan of the high school athletics. Now I could see where they got that from.

"What can I do for you?" he asked.

"Mrs. Simpson told me to come here because I said a cuss word in her class. She said I can't come back until I write a letter apologizing to everyone."

"What was the word you used?"

"Sir?"

"What was the word you used and in what context did you use it?"

"I told a kid to go to hell."

"And in that context, is 'hell' appropriate language for an institution of higher learning?"

"I guess not."

"And from what I'm hearing, you not only used inappropriate language in an institution of higher learning, but you also went after a student, trying to provoke a fight," he said. "Am I correct?"

"I wouldn't say I was trying to provoke a fight."

"What were you trying to do?"

"Get him to shut up," I said.

"And you feel you have the right to decide when someone talks?"

I knew where this was going, so I decided to not even try to defend my actions. "No, sir."

"Good. So, since you did disrupt the class and interfered with other people learning, I will suspend you for one day. Before you are allowed back into school, I will need those letters for Mrs. Simpson. And you will not be allowed to play in the first quarter of the game on Friday."

"Mr. Jacks, it's the championship," I said with a frown, as if this little man had completely lost his mind.

"Ask me if I care."

I could feel my blood boiling. I wanted to reach across that desk and grab his little throat and squeeze, but I exercised a little self-control.

"I will give you a slight break," he said with a grunt. "Since the day has just begun, I will count today as your day for suspension. You are welcome to return tomorrow."

"Mr. Jacks, is there anything else I can do instead of sitting out on Friday? Clean the school building, toilets, cut the grass? Something! Anything!"

"No, I have to send a message to you athletes who have a sense of entitlement. Granted, you're not one of the regular troublemakers, but I've never been one to show favoritism. Now, Romeo, I realize you work hard on the things you've accomplished. But you are also going to be held to a higher standard. You will not pay one dime for college, Mr. Braxton. People will give you things, just because you can throw a football. You are the face of this school, Romeo. Like it or not, you are Tucker. But let's be very clear: You don't run Tucker—I do. Do you understand?"

"I'm not trying to run Tucker," I said.

"Good, then the next time you feel like you can use that language in my school, you'll think twice," he said, his Napoleon complex oozing from every pore.

There was a knock on the door. Then the door opened without an invite from Mr. Jacks. In walked Willie.

"How many days you gonna suspend me for? I'm tired of sitting on that damn bench, man. Let me know so I can get on 'bout my business."

"Go back to class, Willie. Suspending you would be doing you a favor."

"Man," Willie said with a frown as he turned and walked out of the office.

"He just cussed right in front of you."

"Like I said, you don't run Tucker—I do," Mr. Jacks said, hitting himself in the chest so hard he coughed.

I shook my head and shifted from one foot to the other.

"Think before you act, Romeo. And you're lucky I don't have you write an apology to everyone in the school for your actions. To whom much is given, much is expected," he said with a smile.

I nodded my head and waited to be excused.

"See you tomorrow," he said.

I walked out of the man's office just as the bell rang for classes to change.

As I was leaving the office, I bumped into Coach Planter. He had obviously gotten the word that I was in trouble.

"What's going on?" he asked.

"I can't play the first quarter on Friday," I said.

"Why?"

"I got in trouble for cussing in class. I'm suspended for today."

"What the . . ."

"Yeah," I said, waiting for him to punch me in the chest, but he started looking around. "Who suspended you?"

"I did," Mr. Jacks said as he walked past.

"Have you lost your rabbit mind, man?" Coach Planter said, approaching the principal as if he were going to pick him up and toss him across the school. "Man, we're tryna win a state championship. Do you hear me? The state. No-body has time to play these little games with you. We know you're the boss around here, so you don't have to go and ruin the boy's life just so you can prove how bad you think you are."

Mr. Jacks stopped and turned to face the coach.

"You say one more word to me in front of these students and you won't be coaching at all on Friday."

Coach Planter looked at his boss, giving him a "you better be lucky we are in front of these kids" look, but he bit his tongue.

"Go on home, Romeo," he said. "I'll see you tomorrow."

"Sorry, Coach," I said.

"There's nothing to be sorry for. If you suspend every kid who cussed, we'd have about three people in here, but don't worry about it."

"I'd like to see you in my office, Coach Planter," Mr. Jacks said.

"I don't care what you would like. I'm going to the district on you. And I will coach on Friday, because you don't have the authority to make that call," Coach said before walking away.

"We'll see about that," Mr. Jacks said with that ugly smile.

"Yes, we will," Coach Planter shot back. "Yes, we will. You have crossed the line. Romeo is an honor roll student—never even had a warning—and now you wanna throw the book at him just because you don't like the man you see in the mirror. Yes, we will see, you little pathetic piece of—"

"Have a good day, Coach Planter," Mr. Jacks said.

I walked out of the office and straight out of the building.

Amir came running up to me. "What happened, man? I heard you beat up Carlos."

I just shook my head. "Where did you hear that? I never touched him."

"Well, what happened? Come on, Rome. You gotta be smarter than that. You know Carlos ain't nothing but a hater."

"You're right. I got suspended and I can't play in the first quarter on Friday."

"What?" Amir screamed. "Man, we gonna lose."

"Nah, we'll be a'ight," I said, feeling worse by the second. "I'll see you later, bro. I gotta get home and tell Nana what happened."

"A'ight, man," Amir said, looking as if he was more disappointed than I was. "You keep your head up, Rome."

"Come holla at me when you get out of school."

"A'ight, Rome," he said.

I turned around as I crossed the street and noticed Amir was still standing there looking at me. I decided to take the long walk home versus catching the bus. I needed time to think. My mind went all over the place as I walked the two and a half miles to the Village. When I walked in the door, Nana was sitting on the sofa laughing at an old rerun of *Sanford and Son*.

"What are you doing home? Are you feeling okay?" she asked, obviously reading the look on my face.

"Yes, ma'am. I'm okay," I said. "I got suspended from school."

"Suspended?"

"Yes."

"For what?"

"Cussing in class."

"Romeo," she said, standing up. "Cussing? Boy, what's gotten into you? Oh, never mind. I ain't 'bout to let you worry me and get my pressure up. You ain't never gave me an ounce of trouble in all your days, but lately you been getting on my doggone nerves. Clean up that kitchen and then get to your homework."

"Yes, ma'am," I said as I made my way into the kitchen to do as I was told.

9

KWAME

I couldn't contain my excitement. For the first time in two years, I experienced true joy in my heart. I packed up my books and other personal items and placed them in a box. In the two years I had been away, I had read almost two hundred books. Mostly fiction but quite a few nonfiction titles as well. I knew everything there was to know about Barack Obama. Reading had become my escape. When I opened a book, I was no longer prisoner number 345342; I was whoever I wanted to be. I visited faraway places in my mind and experienced new and exciting events.

"What you gonna do with all of your books, man?" Mickey, my cellmate, said.

"Donate them to the library, I guess. I'm not taking one thing from this place. I even had my brother send me some new underwear," I said. "I'm not walking out of here with one thing to remind me of this joint."

Mickey was a quiet and easygoing kid. The guards

placed him with me, because they knew he would be safe
and left alone. I wasn't the type of guy to harass anyone.
And being that Mickey came from a wealthy background,
the administration knew the parasites would have a field
day sucking him dry. They would have his people on the
outside world sending him two thousand dollars per
month for protection.

Mickey was an interracial kid with long curly hair. I told
him to cut it off so as not to attract attention to himself
and he did. He was only seventeen and was sentenced to
ten years with no chance of parole for a carjacking. Though
he had been born into wealth, too much BET had him
caught up in a ghetto fantasy, and now he was paying a
heavy price for trying to copycat some dumb rapper.

"You can take what you want, and I'll donate the rest to
the library," I said, feeling a bit sorry for the little guy. He
was going to have to stand tall without me having his back.

Mickey jumped up and grabbed a few books.

"All of that other stuff is yours too," I said, pointing at
all of the toiletries, snacks, and other personal items I had
piled up in my locker.

"You serious, man?" Mickey said.

"Yeah, man. What am I going to do with it?"

"I mean, you can sell that stuff and make you a few
hundred dollars right quick."

"Nah," I said. "You keep it. My lawyer is waiting for me.
I gotta roll."

"I can't believe you're outta here, cuz," Mickey said.
"I'm happy for you, but I'll be honest—I'm scared, man.
Who's gonna look out for me?"

"You're going to look out for yourself. You already
know what you need to do. Stand tall. Don't let anyone

push you around. Don't ever back down. Not even an inch. You gotta be a little crazy to hold it down up in here. Stay up."

I shook my old cellmate's hand and walked away. I didn't look back until I was on the other side of those stifling walls.

"You ready?" Mrs. Ross said as she met me with a big smile.

"You have no idea," I said, getting in the backseat of her chauffeur-driven town car.

"Where are your belongings?"

"I gave everything away. I don't want anything from that place, not even the memories. Unfortunately, I think it'll be a while before I can get rid of them."

"I understand. Well, welcome to a new start," she said.

"Thanks." I looked around at freedom for the first time in far too long.

The car rolled out of the gates and we were gone.

"Are you hungry?"

"Yes, but I'll wait to get some of my nana's cooking."

"Okay," she said. "Romeo always brags about how good your nana's cooking is. Maybe I'll get an invite to a Sunday dinner one day."

"Anytime," I said. "You can join us anytime. You don't even have to call—just pop in. She's the type who cooks with love, and once you taste some of her sweet-potato pie, you'll never be the same." I closed my eyes, savoring the imaginary taste of my nana's magic.

"Okay," she said. "I'm going to hold you to it."

"Please do," I said, turning my attention to the world as we drove along busy Moreland Avenue.

Mrs. Ross left me to my own thoughts as she pulled out

her BlackBerry and began typing away. I continued to stare out the window at all of the beautiful faces of the people who were going about their lives. I was heartbroken all over again when I thought about how much I had lost. I couldn't believe I had spent one second in prison, especially for something I didn't do, let alone two years.

"Are you going to try to get this conviction removed from my record?"

"Yes," Mrs. Ross said. "We'll have to be granted an appeal, win that appeal, then try to get it expunged. Could get costly."

"Why do they try to make it so hard? I mean, even the prosecutor told me his case against me was pretty weak. He told me that I needed new counsel."

"I'll tell you what I told your brother—prisons are big business, and it's a lot deeper than you young men think it is. The state's largest revenue provider is its prison system. The justice system isn't about guilt or innocence. I'm sure you know why there are more lower-income people in prison than wealthy ones. Money, plain and simple. If you had been fortunate enough to have the money for a good attorney, you wouldn't be here today. You weren't convicted because you were guilty; you were convicted because you were too poor to pay for justice."

"So what can a poor guy do?"

"You're still a very young man, Kwame. Go the extra mile to stay away from bad people and places and anything that might remotely hinder you from removing yourself from the poor category. You have to play the game of chess with this thing called life. Always think three or four moves ahead of your competitor. Because, trust me, they are thinking of all kinds of creative ways to fill those prison walls with bodies."

Mrs. Ross's words were very real to me. I knew what she was saying was true. I had just experienced it, and, of course, the inmates said that every day, but to hear it from someone in her position made it real.

"I didn't grow up with a silver spoon in my mouth, but I worked hard to get where I am. I have a hundred more clients just like you, and when they are taken care of, there will be another hundred waiting for justice."

"How can you afford to keep doing this work without getting paid?"

"I get paid," she said with a smile. "And you, my friend, will get a big fat bill once you get to where you are going in life."

I smiled as I thought she could get every dime I would ever make if it meant me never having to see the inside of a prison again.

"You can pay me back by being successful and being a good role model to kids who need one."

"That's a deal," I said as we pulled up in front of the Village Apartments.

"Thank you so much," I said as I stepped out of the car. "Do you wanna come in and see Nana?"

"I don't have time. But I will definitely make it back soon. After all, a girl has to eat."

10

ROMEO

I hated playing in the rain. The ball was always slippery, and even with screw-in cleats, it was almost impossible to get any decent traction on the soggy field. We were down by a field goal, but we had the ball on our own forty-yard line. Less than a minute to go in the game and our coach called a 31 fake, 28 option wild blast. In football talk, that meant I was going to fake the ball to the halfback coming through the one hole, and the tailback and I were going to roll out to the right where I had the option to keep the ball or pitch it to the tailback.

Outside of the rain, it didn't get any better than this. Even the rain made it somewhat fun. We were facing our archrival, and I was facing my childhood nemesis, Ricky Baxter. I had to give it up to the guy—Ricky was a beast. He had already sacked me twice tonight, and each time he called me some name that my nana definitely wouldn't approve of. We had played against each other throughout our lives, and word on the street was he hated me. I didn't really know him, but the feeling was mutual. But I couldn't deny his skills. He was just as highly recruited by colleges as I was, and lots of people said he was the best player in the state. I thought he was good but the best in the state? Nah, that title belonged to none other than yours truly, so now I had to show him what all the hype was about.

I walked up behind the center, bent my knees, and placed my hands under the center's butt. I saw Ricky creeping up to the line; then he backed off. He yelled something to his players. The other linebacker shifted to his left, and Ricky shifted over to the right where I would be running. He read the play. I don't know how he knew what was coming, but he knew. I could see it in his eyes. Normally I would have called an audible and changed the play at the line of scrimmage, but not this time. I wanted this challenge. I was going right at him. I called my cadence.

Down!

Set!

Hut!

Hut!

I felt the ball touch my hands, and I dropped back, turned around, and carried out my fake, rolling around the right side of the field with the ball in both hands. I could see the saliva dripping from Ricky's mouth through his face mask as he barreled toward me. He was coming with the speed of a freight train. I knew right then there was no way I was pitching that ball to our tailback, Christian. I was going to go straight at Ricky. I could already feel the impact of me trucking right over him. I visualized him flying back as I stepped on his chest and took the ball the length of the field for a touchdown. Even though Christian seemed to have a clear path up the sideline toward an easy victory, I needed a little payback. This fool had sacked me twice and called me a few dirty names. All of this went through my head in a matter of milliseconds. I was running hard, and everything seemed to be moving in slow motion. Ricky was coming at me and I was going at him. I guess he wanted to prove to me that he was the best player in the state, because his eyes said he would love nothing more than to send me out of this game on a stretcher. I wasn't about to let that happen. He would be the one paramedics carried out. Just as he was close enough for me to hear him growl, I pitched the ball off to Christian. At the last second, I lowered my shoulder pad and caught him in the chest, creating a devastating collision between myself and the hard-hitting Ricky. He went flying and so did I. I heard him grunt as my helmet hit the unprotected area above his shoulder pads and beneath his helmet. We both hit the ground with a thud. I rolled over and saw Christian's number 22 jersey racing up the sideline, taking us to victory.

My center and offensive tackle, each weighing almost three hundred pounds, ran over and snatched me off the ground as if I were a rag doll. They lifted me up on their massive shoulders and carried me around to celebrate our victory. Through all of the jubilation and chaos, I turned and saw him standing on the other side of the fence. I tapped both of my teammates and asked them to let me down. My heart was already racing, but after seeing my brother, it increased a little more.

"Kwame!" I yelled, hopping down and running over to where he was standing. I couldn't get to him quick enough. My wide smile was met by an even wider one coming from him. Seeing my big brother standing on the grass made the victory I just experienced seem like nothing. Having him home was the real victory. I reached over the fence and hugged him for the first time in two years. I didn't want to let him go. He patted me on the back.

"Not bad, youngster," he said as we released each other from our bear hug. "You looked good out there."

"When did you come home?"

"Not even two hours ago."

"Did you see Nana yet?"

He shook his head. "No, I went by the house, but she wasn't home. So I figured this was where you guys would be."

"She's here," I said, pointing in the direction of where our grandmother was sitting. "Even though she's probably trying to get outta here by now."

"Okay," he said, smiling from ear to ear. "Go ahead and enjoy yourself with your teammates. I'll catch you at home a little later."

"You wanna ride the bus with us?" I said, smiling from ear to ear. "Coach got suspended for tonight's game. He got into it with the principal over me, but he's here."

"What did you do?"

"Cussed in class. I didn't play the first quarter, but when I got in there, I did my thing. I heard the University of Southern California scouts are here."

"Oh, yeah. Well maybe they can teach you how to watch your mouth in school," Kwame said with a smile.

"Come on. Ride the bus," I urged him. "I know Coach would love to see you."

"Nah, tell him I said hello. I need to go and find Nana."

"Okay, man," I said, not wanting to take my eyes off of

him for fear that I was dreaming. "Man, I'm glad you're home."

I turned to leave but stopped and turned back to my brother, who was still staring at me. "Kwame."

"Yeah."

"I bet you didn't do it like me?" I said with a wink.

"You're right. I would've run him over and still scored," he said with a wink of his own.

"Team player, baby," I said, slapping the tiger logo on the front of my jersey. "That's me all day."

"I hear you, team player. Go on and get with your boys. I'm home now. We'll catch up later tonight."

I balled up my fist and gave him a pump before running back to join my teammates. Just as I crossed midfield, I heard my name being called. I turned around and saw Ricky running my way.

"Good game, cuzzo," he said, extending the huge paw he had for a hand.

"Same to you," I said, shaking his hand.

"All these years and we never even said one word to each other," he said, pulling me in for a brotherly hug.

"Yeah." I patted his back. "Kind of crazy, right?"

"Yeah, it is. You played a real good game, man."

"Thanks, bro. So did you."

"You picked a school yet?"

"Not yet," I said. "Have you?"

"I'm headed to Georgia. I signed a letter of intent last night."

"Whoa. That's what's up. Georgia's up there on my list too."

"Man, come on down to Athens and let's wreck shop. You handle that O, and I'll lock down the D."

"I might just do that," I said, nodding my head.

"Man, I thought you were gonna keep that ball," he said, shaking his head at the missed opportunity. "Augh," he growled.

"Thought about it," I said, and reached out and touched those cannons he had for biceps. "Decided I would rather live to see another day."

"Ha-ha. You seem like an a'ight dude, Romeo. Everybody told me you were a butt wipe."

I smiled, then laughed. "I heard the same thing about you, playa. Just goes to show you can't listen to everything you hear."

"No doubt. Well, let me get on back over there with the crew. I hope to see you down at Georgia, cuzzo."

I smiled and slapped his hand again. Someone called our names, and we turned to face a guy with a trash bag over his head and his camera equipment.

"Can I get a shot of you guys?" he said.

We turned and faced the guy. I held up one finger and Ricky acted as if he was choking me.

After the guy had his picture, we said our good-byes. I ran off to celebrate a little more with my fellow Tucker Tigers. Just as I was catching up to the last guy who was walking into the locker room, I noticed another familiar face and stopped.

"You didn't think I was gonna make it, huh?" my mother said calmly. She had changed clothes and even looked like she'd taken a shower.

"No, I didn't. But I'm glad you did," I said, truly surprised to see her.

"You're pretty good, little boy." She pinched my cheek like she used to do when I was little.

"Thanks," I replied.

"Your father was a quarterback too. He wasn't as good as you or Kwame, but I can tell where you guys get it from."

My father! That was a word that I couldn't ever remember hearing Pearl mention. I didn't know what to say to that one. I was still awestruck with the way my mother was acting and looking. It was as if a real decent woman had taken control of her body and was making her act as if she was a caring and supportive mother.

We shared a silent but awkward moment before she broke the ice.

"I just wanted to say hi to you before I get out of here," she said before turning and walking away.

"Hey," I called out. She stopped and looked back at me. "Why don't you come by the apartment tonight? Somebody wants to see you."

"Maybe tomorrow," she said with sad eyes. "I gotta go to work tonight."

"Okay," I said, wondering why she was holding on to that lie. "Well, drop by tomorrow, then."

She nodded, then disappeared into the night. I stood there watching her until I couldn't even see her shadow. This was crazy. Who was that woman? And how could we get her to be around all the time?

11

ROMEO

Nana cooked one of the biggest meals I'd ever seen. Anyone peeking through our window would've thought it was a Sunday afternoon instead of late Friday. Try as we might to get her to relax and get some rest after a long day, she wasn't hearing it. Kwame was home, and no amount of persuasion was going to stop her from cooking his favorite dishes.

"If this little knotty-headed rascal right here would've told me you were coming home, I would've had it ready for you," she said with a wide smile as she pinched my cheek.

"I wanted to surprise you," I said, just as happy.

"You know I don't like surprises. I'm too old for surprises. I'll have a heart attack fooling round with you, Romeo."

I couldn't remember the last time I'd seen my grandmother this happy. And seeing my nana like this made me feel like the world was a beautiful place.

We ate and chatted about any and everything that came to mind until our hearts were content and our bellies were full, which was somewhere close to midnight. Kwame and I took care of the dishes while Nana put the many leftovers away. She hugged both of us before retiring to her room. We headed back to our bedroom and got in a little brother-to-brother time.

"How's Ngiai doing?" Kwame asked as he plopped down on his bed.

"I don't know. She cut me off," I said as I lay on my back staring at the ceiling.

"What did you do?" Kwame asked.

"Why do you assume I did something?"

"Because you said she cut you, which means you messed up."

"I got caught cheating."

"How you get caught cheating? You shouldn't cheat if you don't know how to do it," he said, laughing.

"Man, this old skank named Vonetta running around telling everybody she's pregnant by me. Word got back to Ngiai, and, well, after that it was a wrap."

Kwame leaned up with his elbows on his knees. "So is she?"

"No."

"How do you know that for sure?" he asked.

"I had on a condom," I said.

"You shouldn't be focused on sex right now, Rome. You have the rest of your life to get some. Right now you need to be focused on getting somewhere. Let me tell you something I heard somewhere from somebody: You will never miss out on women chasing money, but you will miss out on a whole lot of money chasing women."

"Man, I ain't chasing nobody. They're chasing me."

"Yeah, okay. It's the same thing, little boy. Get your mind right is all I'm saying."

"Okay, Pop," I said with a smile.

Kwame smiled and relaxed a little. I looked over at him and saw he was shaking his head. Then he started laughing. He laughed so hard that he had to hold his side. I looked at him like he had taken some of that stuff our mother had gotten into.

"What's so funny, man?"

He continued to laugh. Nana knocked on the wall, which was a sign for us to tone it down.

"I don't see what's so funny. You laughing at me because Ngiai cut me?"

"Nah, I'm not laughing at you, Rome. Just having a moment, man. I still can't believe I'm sitting here on this bed talking to you. I thought this day would never come."

"Well, I'm glad you're home. You know I did that time with you, right? Nana did it too."

"I know," he said, dropping his head. "I wish I could say I was sorry, but, man, that was the craziest thing. I've never committed the slightest of crimes. Never even stole a piece of bubble gum and yet there I was in the mix with some of the worst people you'd ever want to meet. I kept asking God what he was trying to teach me. I still haven't gotten an answer."

I sat up on my bed and faced my brother.

"I guess in due time I'll know why I went through that," he said.

"Hey, Kwame. Did you see Pearl at the game?"

"Nah," he said nonchalantly. "How she doing?"

"Not too good. At least she doesn't look too good. Even

though she looked better tonight than she has in years, she still looked jacked up. She claims she's working, but I can't see how. She came over here the other day looking like one of those people in that old Michael Jackson video. I don't know what's going on with her."

"So she's still out there smoking her problems away?" he asked.

"I guess. Something's strange about her, though. Not just the drugs. Something about her seems off."

"Drugs will make you seem a little off, little bro."

"General Mack was out there talking about he saw her with some bad people."

"What kind of bad people?" Kwame said with a frown and his eyebrows raised.

"I don't know. You know how General Mack is, but there's gotta be something to it."

"Yeah, well, you gotta be careful about dealing with addicts. I mean, she's Mom and all, but her loyalties are to those drugs, and until that changes, you gotta keep your eyes wide open or just stay away from her."

"I know, but like I said, something just didn't seem right," I said. Then I remembered something. I jumped up and ran to my closet and came back with the roll of money Wicked had given me.

"Wicked told me to give you this," I said, handing it to him.

Kwame stared at it for a minute, then reached out and grabbed it.

"I guess this is his guilt gift," he said with a huff.

"Whatchu mean?"

"Nothing," he said, fanning me away.

"Did Wicked have something to do with you going to prison?"

"Nah," he said, but I knew he wasn't sharing the entire story. He seemed different. Prison had taken away his innocence. There was a hardness to him that I wasn't used to.

"So what's up with college? Who's looking at you?"

"Lots of people, man," I said as I retrieved two shoe boxes filled with recruiting letters. "Schools out West are even sending me letters. I have a handwritten one from Nick Saban, but I don't think I'm going to Alabama."

"You might wanna take one of those West Coast schools up on their offer. You need to get far away from here, man."

"Why does everybody keep saying that? I mean, Georgia has some of the best schools in the country, and people come from all over the world to go to them. And here I am, right in the city already and everybody wants me to leave. I don't get it."

"It's because you're from here, so it's not the same for you. You know the nooks and crannies of the city, and believe it or not, a lot of the people who smile in your face will be the first ones to stab you in the back. Plus, getting away makes you grow up. You can't run home to Nana just because you're hungry or you want your clothes washed. You gonna have to learn how to do those things on your own. Going away might be the best thing for you."

"I ain't tryna go too far," I said.

"Look at you. Why? You'll miss being able to hang on to Nana's skirts?"

"You the same way," I said.

"Let's think hard about this school thing, Romeo," Kwame said as he lay back on the bed.

"What about you? What are your plans?"

"I gotta get a job, man."

"You can go to school and get your degree."

"I don't know," he said, closing his eyes.

"Maybe we need to think hard on that one too," I said.

I looked over at my brother and heard a light snore coming from his bed. A smile crept across my face. That sound drove me crazy when we were little. So much so that I would get up and crawl into bed with Nana, but now it was the sweetest sound in the world, and I couldn't think of another place I would rather be.

12

KWAME

The screams were loud and clear. Some poor soul was "getting adjusted" to life on the inside and was losing his mind in the process. Every night after lights-out, the screams would start. Sometimes it was someone struggling to keep his manhood; other times it was someone just going plum crazy. It's amazing how I learned to find sleep among all the chaos. The first night was the hardest. I was standing in my cell when the so-called welcoming crew came to pay me a visit. Someone snuck up behind me and wrapped a large bicep around my neck while another joker punched me in the stomach. I kicked the guy in front of me with everything I had and shot an elbow to the guy choking me. The guy behind me let go, and I tried to break his face with my fist. The guy I kicked got up and ran screaming for a guard. After that, word got around that I was not an easy target.

A cell door slammed. I popped up on my bed and looked around.

Where am I?

I jumped up and tripped over something on the floor. I caught myself on the dresser.

"You okay, man?" a strangely familiar voice said.

I zeroed in on the face that was slightly illuminated by the streetlight. All of a sudden, I felt a rage deep inside of me.

"Why you screaming? Who's messing with you?" I growled.

"Kwame, calm down, man. I'm not screaming. I'm okay. It's me, Romeo," my little brother said.

Reality started setting in and I realized my little brother had not joined me in prison, and he was not in danger. It was just a dream.

"You a'ight, man?" Romeo asked.

I sat on the side of the bed and took a few deep breaths to clear my head. "I guess I gotta get used to being home." I chuckled. "What time is it?"

"It's"—he fumbled with the clock—"three o'clock in the morning, man."

"Sorry to wake you up, bro. Go back to sleep," I said, lying back down myself.

I lay on my back and looked out the window. The streetlight gave me just enough visibility to see my little brother. He had already drifted back off. I tossed and turned for another ten or fifteen minutes before I gave up on sleep. I used the streetlight to find my pants and sneakers.

I eased out of the bedroom and crossed the living room floor. I stopped when I heard the floor creak beneath my weight. I stayed still for a minute, hoping I didn't wake Nana.

"Where you going, baby?"

So much for not waking her.

"I'm going out for a few minutes. Can't sleep. I need to get some fresh air."

"Well, open a window. Nothing good out there this time of night, or should I say morning," Nana said.

I walked over and wrapped my arms around my grandmother. She was so sweet, and I could see the worry in her eyes.

"I can't stay in the house forever, Nana. I'm not gonna get into any trouble."

"Just promise me you'll stay away from that boy. Anybody with a name like Wicked gots to be close kin to the Devil."

"I promise," I said, kissing her forehead as I lied.

I opened the front door and closed it as quietly as I could. The night air felt good on my skin. I inhaled and exhaled the essence of my beautiful ghetto. For the last twenty-four months, I hadn't been able to get up and take a walk when I wanted to, but now I could and I planned to take full advantage of it. I stood there for what must've been five full minutes, looking around the grounds that I'd called home for so long. Even at three in the morning, the ghetto still showed signs of life. The night crawlers were out in full force, getting their hustles on.

"Soldier," a loud voice boomed, scaring the crap out of me.

"What up, General Mack?" I said with a smile.

"Get at attention, soldier," he commanded with a straight face. "What's wrong with you? You done lost your rabbit mind. I'm the general."

"General," I said, reaching out to touch both of his

shoulders. "I don't know if anyone has ever told you this before, but you are out of the army and I never joined."

The general's eyes bulged out of his head; he furrowed his brows, looked at his clothes, and smiled. "As you were, boy. I'm a soldier. Always has been and always will be. Now stand down. At ease," he barked so loud that you would think it was three in the afternoon instead of the morning.

"You are going to wake everybody up in this building."

"Good," he snapped just as loud. "Nothing comes to a sleeper but a dream."

I chuckled at the sight before me. While I had been away, I had often thought of General Mack and his crazy ways.

"How was life in the stockade?" he asked.

"The what?"

"The clink, the brig. Jail, boy," General Mack said.

"How do you think it was?"

"I wouldn't know. I'm a law-abiding citizen," he said.

"Have you seen Wicked?"

"Nope, but I guess if you looking for that fool, then you must've enjoyed your state-sponsored vacation at Fort Leavenworth."

"Nah, and I wasn't in Leavenworth. It's nothing like that. I just wanna holla at him."

"Look over by the basketball courts. That seems to be where the lowlifes like to congregate. I guess they can get a jump on the kids that way."

"Okay, General Mack. You take care of yourself and try not to shoot anybody."

"I seen yo momma," he said, pausing for effect. "And things ain't right with her. You a man?"

"What?"

"Did I stutter? I asked if you were a man."

"Of course I'm a man."

"Well, then, act like one and get your momma straight."

"Where did you see her?"

"I gave yo lil brother the intel. Told the boy to do a follow-up. What's wrong with him? Tell him I'm about to bring him up on dereliction-of-duty charges and have him court-martialed. Maybe a little time in the stockade will put some pep in his step," General Mack said with a frown as if he were really in a position to send my little brother any-where.

"Okay, General. I'll talk to Rome and I'ma get my mom straight," I said, trying to move on with my night.

"That's yo momma I'm talking about, not some broad off the block. I don't care what people think of her. That's still your momma."

"I'm on it," I said, giving him the required salute.

"Attention," he said loud enough to wake up everybody. He slapped his hands to his sides again and returned my salute. Then, as if he heard a strange sound that only his crazy ears could hear, his eyes darted from side to side. He stooped down real low and crawled around the building as if the enemy was near and he was going to sneak up on them. I stood there watching our resident nutcase as he disappeared out of sight and into the night.

13

KWAME

I walked around our complex with an easy stroll. I couldn't stop thinking about how good it felt to be home. I stopped, looked up at the sky, and thanked God for my freedom. Not much had changed since I'd been away. With the exception of a fence being up around the area, everything was the same.

I passed by a familiar face and paused. "My God" was all I could say. How I hoped that my eyes were not lying to me.

"No. Please, say it ain't so," I said to myself before turning around and realizing that my eyes were not lying.

Mora, the object of all my adolescent affection, was looking a complete mess. She was standing with a man who was scratching his arm as if he had just been bitten by an army of mosquitoes. But anybody who knew the streets knew that it wasn't the insects that had him scratching; it was the drug monkey that was causing his discomfort.

"Hey, Kwame," Mora said, as if nothing was out of the ordinary with her condition. "How you doing, baby?"

"Hey, Mora. How are you doing?" I said.

"Mora," the tall man called as she walked over to me. "Ask him. And hurry up."

Mora nodded at the man and made a face for him to shut up. Then she turned to me and smiled. "I'm good."

I didn't respond. I was still trying to come to grips with how a straight-A student who graduated at the top of her high school class could end up going down the road to destruction.

"Kwame, let me hold something. I know you got it. You look like a million bucks, always did," she said, trying to butter me up with compliments.

"Hold what, Mora?" I said, looking at her while my heart broke into a million little pieces.

"A few dollars. I know you got it. Don't play stingy with me 'cause I know you got it. You big money. Pockets stay swole. Let your girl hold something. I'll wash your car or something, but I ain't no crack chick, so keep your mind out the gutter," she said.

"I don't need you to do anything," I said, reaching in my pocket and pulling out a five-dollar bill. Before I could say a word more, Mora snatched the money from my hand and ran off with her addict of a friend. I stood there and watched as another potential-filled friend drifted off into the abyss.

I looked around at the apartment buildings and suddenly realized that life was hard. Nana had always insulated us from real ghetto living, but now I saw it up front and in living color. Only the strong survived. The more I thought about it, the more I started to have thoughts of being a vessel for change. But what could I do? I wasn't sure, but I knew I couldn't sit back idly while good people threw their lives away.

A big white BMW pulled into the parking lot beside the basketball courts and parked. The courts were where you could always find the hustlers and street types. The kids had long ago stopped playing ball there because of the stray bullets and drug activity.

A fat dude jumped out of the fancy car and huddled up with a few guys who were standing along the benches on the basketball court. I walked toward them and caught the stare of one of the youngsters.

"Nah, homes. You can't walk through here. Grown-man business going down." Some clown seeking attention approached me with his arm extended to keep me at bay.

I didn't miss a stride.

The clown rushed over and stopped directly in front of me with his hand close to his waist. I guess he wanted me to know he had a gun, but I had just left a place where real killers roamed, and I could see the coward in this guy's eyes from a mile away. He was nothing but a fly waiting to be swatted away.

I stopped walking and stared at the bony little fella, who couldn't have been any older than sixteen.

"You got a death wish, homie?" he snapped in a deep New Orleans accent. "I told you to slow your roll, but you wanna be disrespectful."

"Boo!" I said, jumping at him, causing him to flinch back. He fiddled around with his gun before dropping it on the blacktop.

Laughter erupted from behind him. Then I heard my name being yelled.

"Kwame!" Wicked screamed like a kid at Christmastime as he hustled his big body over to me.

All of the other guys were doubled over laughing at the wannabe tough guy and his poor attempt at intimidation.

Wicked picked me up in a bear hug and swung me around. "I missed ya, baby boy," he yelled at the top of his lungs.

"Man, put me down," I said. "And stop all of that yelling before you wake up the dead."

"I missed ya, boy," he said again, stepping back to take a look at me.

"I see," I said, not feeling the same way about him.

Wicked stared at me for a few more seconds, then shook his head. "My goodness. Lil bro told me you were on your way back to the world." He smiled, showing off a mouth full of platinum- and diamond-covered teeth.

"What is that mess in your mouth?"

"Success, baby," he said, reaching into his pocket and pulling out a large roll of money. He slapped the money into my hand. "That's you. And it ain't nothing but a small deposit on what I owe you."

I slipped the money into my pocket and turned my attention to the guy who had approached me.

"How old are you, boy?"

"Fifteen," said the light-complexioned skinny boy who had a million tattoos covering both of his skinny arms.

"And how long have you been a gangster?"

"What?"

"How long have you been a gangster?" I asked again.

"I ain't no gangster," he said. "I'm just me."

"You're a security guard?"

"No," he said with a frown. "You see a badge and a flashlight?"

"Then what are you?"

"I just told you. I'm me."

"Who is 'me'? I mean, I wasn't bothering you. I was just taking a walk. Why in the world would you wanna pull a gun on somebody who's out and about minding his own business?"

"I'm just saying," he said, hunching his shoulders. "I told you to stop but you ignored me."

"What? So you own these courts? Was I trespassing on your property or something?"

"I'm just doing my job," the boy said.

"And what is your job? Harassing people? So you're saying that if you live in the apartments, you can't take a walk? Little idiots like you running around with guns make things bad for everybody. Now what are you going to do?"

He looked around with a confused look on his face.

"I'm waiting," I said.

"Apologize, punk," Wicked spat as if he knew exactly where this line of questioning was going.

"Oh. Sorry," the youngster said.

"Apology accepted, but what else are you going to do?"

He looked around to his friends for a clue as to what I was talking about.

"Okay, let me help you. You are going to give me your gun. Then you're going to take your narrow little behind in the house. When you wake up in the morning, you're going to get a trash bag and clean up all of this mess you see lying around here. And when you get done, you are going to come find me so I can find something else constructive you can do with your time."

"You got jokes," the boy said. "And you real funny."

"Do I look like I'm laughing?"

"I mean . . . I see that you my man's friend and all. I can respect that. But, homeboy, you ain't my daddy." The idiot frowned, fanning me off.

"That ain't what you want, fella," Wicked warned. "Trust me on that one. Get the trash bag and be done with it. That ain't a snake you wanna tangle with."

"You're right. I'm not your daddy. If you had a daddy worth his spit, then I wouldn't have to try and teach you how to conduct yourself, now, would I?"

"Man, my daddy is dead. Keep his name outta your mouth," he said, standing up ready to fight.

"Okay, we can do this two different ways. You can just do what I told you to do, or you can do what I told you to do with a few cracked ribs and a black eye. But you will do what I ask, lil homie." I held out my hand. "Gun."

The idiot looked around for some kind of support from his cronies. When he got none, he reluctantly handed me the gun. I took the little gun, a blatant violation of my parole, and placed it in my pants, at the small of my back. I would have given it to Wicked, but he would only hand it off to another little uninformed youngster to continue the destruction. I planned to throw it away the first chance I got.

"What's your name?"

"Frank," he mumbled.

"Nice to meet you, Frank," I said, extending my hand.

He looked at my hand for a few seconds, then slapped it.

"I guess no one ever taught you how to shake a man's hand?"

"Man, come on," he said, obviously feeling like I did when General Mack made me stand in front of him while he did his inspection.

I took my hand back and nodded. "Okay, gangster. It's past your bedtime. You got a lot of work to do in the morning."

Frank looked at Wicked, but all he got was a finger pointing in the direction of where Frank lived.

"Your gangster days are over, fella. Are you still in school?" I asked.

"Nope."

"Well, you better brush up on those study skills, because come Monday morning, we're taking a trip over to the high school and see what we can do about putting an end to your dumbness," I said.

Frank laughed me off before walking away. He snuck a few peeks over his shoulder as if I was going to start smiling and tell him the joke was on him. But this was no joke. I was serious about doing something to change things in my hood. One little gangster at a time.

"What's up with you, homie?" Wicked asked. "You done turned into Muslim or something in that penitentiary?"

"Nah."

"I know you done got swole up. Geezus, boy." He touched my arm.

I sighed and looked at Frank as he slowly moved into the darkness. "Nah, man, just tired of seeing young brothers throw their lives away over this façade of thug life. If I can stop somebody from hitting those prison walls, I'ma do it."

"I hear you but, man, you just took away my best help right there," Wicked said with a chuckle. "That was a top earner. He from Nawlins, so you already know how he gets down."

I didn't respond to his ignorance.

"Kwame, I got these streets on lock, brah. I'm making money hand over fist. Now, I know you just got home and you know I owe you big-time for keeping it real. So here's what I propose. You come in with me fifty-fifty off the top and I'll cut all the young boys off. This grown man's business anyway."

I stared at my old homie and felt a twinge of sadness. The sad thing was that he had been conditioned for so long to think that we were supposed to hurt each other by selling drugs to one another that he thought it was okay. I didn't hate him. As much as I wanted to, I didn't have any room in my heart for hate. I was a blessed man, and I was intent on passing along the blessings.

14

KWAME

"Wicked, you're okay with me, but I can't roll with you," I said, folding my arms as I stood in front of him.

"I understand how you feel. I mean, you just got home. Take your time, but come on and get some of this money, brah," he pleaded as if the money he was talking about wasn't destroying an entire generation of people.

"I don't want that kind of money. And you already know I don't function like that."

"Yeah, but you ain't gonna be able to get no legit job with that felony, so why not get this money?" he reasoned.

"I don't blame you for the last two years. Although what you did was foul, I should've known better, so I have only myself to blame."

"Brah, I just had a baby girl, and I know that don't mean a thing at this point, but I figured since you were innocent, there was no way they could convict you."

I frowned at him and tried to peer into his brain to see

if he could really be that naive. "Are you serious? Innocent people get locked up every day," I said. "But look at you, dirty as a pig yet free as a bird. Left out here to continue on with your ill deeds."

"Yeah, I hear you. But you didn't have a problem taking the proceeds from those ill deeds, did you?" Wicked snapped, his attitude changing.

"Oh, not at all," I said, pulling the large roll from my pocket. "This doesn't even begin to pay for what I went through, homie. So here's how you can pay the rest."

"What's that, Malcolm X?" he said after spitting on the ground, letting me know that what I was about to say was going in one of his ears and out the other. But I was gonna say it anyway.

"Take your poison somewhere else. You make a few dollars, but everybody else loses. I've seen too many of our people go into that prison because they were out here clowning like you. Lazy and unprepared. They don't want to work because they are too busy chasing that quick buck, but the funny thing is, once you're incarcerated, all you do is work. And on top of that, you got somebody telling you when to eat, sleep, and take a shower. Man, I wouldn't wish prison on a rabid dog, yet you have little boys out here throwing rocks at the jailhouse, begging to get in. And for what? So they can ride around in a fancy car? Impress some little chicken-head girl? Then what? They get into her pants and impregnate her with another little dummy to take his place after he's shipped off to the can? Come on, man."

Wicked looked up at the clear, dark night as if searching for the right words to say. "Kwame, you've been my dog for a long time, and I understand you been through a lot, but if I don't get this money, then somebody else is gonna get it. You know that. So I respect your decision to keep your hands clean, but this my business, brah. What else am I gonna do?"

"Are you kidding me? Man, you're smarter than me. That's pretty obvious, being that you gave me the business end of that case."

"Come on, man. I know you don't think I set you up?"

"No, I don't think you did, but that's neither here nor there at this point," I said. "The past is the past. Take a look around you, Wicked. Nobody's around here but us, and guess what? This is the exact same way the prisons look. We act a fool and the powerful sit back and smile. We don't even need the Ku Klux Clan anymore. You know why? People like you have taken their place. You've been conditioned to behave like an animal. Why are we glorifying the hood? Who in the world would want to live like this?" I said, pointing to a lady standing about thirty feet away. She was as skinny as a toothpick and high out of her mind. "Look at that," I said. "That just might've been the next Condoleezza Rice, but we're playing her cheap. We help her fail because you need that ten dollars she's gonna pay you for her fix, just so you can drive around in a nice car. Whoopee doppee do."

Wicked leaned back on his car and started clapping. A long, patronizing clap. "My my my, prison sure has made you a dreamer. And let me tell you something. That chick over there ain't ever been close to being no Condoleezza Rice and thank God for it, because Secretary Rice wasn't all that, anyway, if you ask me."

"You see what I'm saying, man. Most of the dudes

around here wouldn't know the first thing about Con-doleezza Rice, much less her job title."

"Whatever, brah. Save that dreaming for your bedroom and wake up and smell the coffee. This the hood. The ghetto. People smoke and people sell. It's all about supply and demand, Kwame X."

"So you just give in to the misery and become part of it?" I asked.

"You do your thing and I'll do mine," Wicked said, balling his fist and placing it in front of me.

I didn't expect Wicked to understand my pain. How could he? He had never walked in my shoes. I tapped his fist with mine and sighed deeply.

"You stay up, Kwame. Glad you home and we'll just have to say I owe you one. And I always pay my debts," Wicked said, starting his car with a remote control before he got in it.

I stood there and watched my old friend wobble his big body into the high-priced automobile. He gave me a plat-inum smile, turned up his music as loud as it would go, and then put his car in reverse and backed out of the proj-ects.

I stood in the middle of the basketball court and looked around. I'd played many games on this court, and I missed it. I saw an old rubber basketball over by the fence and walked over and picked it up. I dribbled it a few times and let one go. *Swish. Some things never change,* I thought.

15

KWAME

Just as the ball went through the net, I heard General Mack yell, "Incoming."

Just as I turned toward his voice, I saw that skinny kid Frank walking at me with a gun extending from his arm and aimed in my direction. The first shot exploded and interrupted the calm of the night. I hit the pavement and rolled over under a steel bench.

Frank was still walking toward me with that gun when General Mack ran at him, barreling him over with the blow of an NFL linebacker. Frank hit the ground as the gun flew from his hand. I jumped up and ran over to the gun. I picked it up and stood over him.

"Get up," I snapped.

"Boy, what's your major malfunction?" General Mack barked, slapping Frank across the back of his head while they were still on the ground.

"So now you wanna kill me?" I asked.

Frank didn't respond. He just laid there breathing hard.

"I guess a cat got your tongue," General Mack said before slapping him again. General stood to his feet and then snatched Frank to his.

"Man, you better keep your old dirty hands offa me." Frank turned to General Mack.

"Or what? You gonna get the taste beat out of your silly mouth?" General Mack said as he jumped into a karate stance. "Make your move, grasshopper. Make your move."

"That's twice tonight you pulled a gun on me. Now, why don't you tell me what it is that I've done to you that has you so determined to kill me?"

"You tried me, man," he said with tears in his eyes.

"I tried you?"

"Yeah," he said plainly.

"So killing somebody is now the price for trying you?"

"You disrespected me, man."

"Wait a minute. I'm minding my business and you pull a gun on me and in your peanut brain, I disrespected you?"

He looked down.

"No, I tried to help you. What kind of life do you think you're going to have hanging out in the wee hours of the morning with Wicked? I just left prison for hanging out with Wicked. So instead of you tryna kill me, you should be thanking me."

"Yeah, dummy," General said, slapping the boy again before jumping back into his stance.

"Touch me again, man." Frank turned to General Mack.

General Mack slapped him again and turned up his head as if daring him to respond, but all Frank did was huff and puff.

"Now is this over? Because if you want to keep playing this little game, we can. I can get just as gangster as the next man," I said. "But that's not gonna get us anywhere. It'll get you a trip to a hospital or maybe the morgue, and maybe I'll get a trip back to the pen. Who wins? Nobody and at the end of the day, when we ask for what, the answer will be 'because he tried me.' "

"Why is your dumb behind dead, boy?" General Mack said in a booming Godlike voice. "Because this guy tried me, God. What is 'tried me,' son? I'm God and I can understand every dialect known to man, but I don't speak the stupid language."

"So is this over, Frank?" I asked.

"We straight," Frank said.

"No, we're not straight. You tried to kill me, idiot. All I'm asking is if you were done tryna shoot me?"

"Whatever, man," Frank said, attitude oozing from his every pore.

"Okay, tough guy, think about it like this. I could call the cops and you could be arrested. You would be charged with attempted murder or at the very least aggravated assault. That's an automatic ten years in prison."

"And in that time, you just might go from Frank to Francine," General Mack said.

I looked Frank up and down. Fresh new sneakers on, pants hanging off his butt, and a T-shirt that was a little too tight. "Now, do you need ten years to think about how much of a dummy you are being right now?"

General Mack started laughing, and then he started marching in place.

"Franky," a loud female's voice screeched. "Franky, what are you doing out here?"

"Nothing," he said.

"Kelli?" I said, straining to see if this was the same woman I once knew.

"Kwame," she said with a hint of recognition on her face. Then she smiled a big pretty smile that almost melted my heart.

I walked over and gave her a hug. "What brings you to my neck of the woods?" I asked.

Kelli was just as gorgeous as she was when we met ten years ago. Her face was a flawless oasis of mahogany. I couldn't stop staring at her. My eyes roamed over her body. She had more curves than Spaghetti Junction. Even in the midst of all of the confusion, she had me thinking how good it would feel to have her in my life again. She had been my girlfriend in eighth grade, until she moved away to New Orleans.

"I moved back here," she said, then her eyes darted over to Frank.

I had to force myself to keep from gawking at her. "So you know this guy?" I asked.

"He my nephew. Came with me from New Orleans. What did he do?"

"Tried to kill me."

"What?" Kelli frowned and slapped Frank so hard I felt sorry for him.

"Pulled a gun on me," I said, reaching for the gun I had in my back. "I took this one from him, but he came back with another one." I showed her the other one.

"Have you lost your mind, boy?" Kelli yelled, going after her nephew again, who was backing up.

I grabbed her and held her back. "Hey, calm down. It's all good," I said.

"No, it's not all good. I'm sick of you, Franky. I'm so tired of your crap that I don't know what to do anymore. I promised my brother that I would take care of you, but you . . . you just insist on being a bum. I'm not gonna be out here running around after you all times of night like you don't have any sense."

"Whatever. I don't need you," Frank said, trying to act hardcore.

"Oh, yeah? Well, we'll see about that," she said.

"Whatever. I'll come and get my stuff," Frank said with all the defiance he could muster.

"And go where?" she asked.

"Don't you worry about it," he shot back.

Kelli growled and balled up her fist.

"This is crazy. I heard gunshots out here, and why did I know you had something to do with it? I come out here and sure enough, here you are right in the middle of it," Kelli said, looking straight at Frank. "You know what? You're not going to be happy until you end up in jail or somebody kills you. But I'm done. I've had it up to here with you," she said, throwing up her hands and storming back to her apartment.

Frank took a half step to follow Kelli, then stopped and looked at me.

"What's up?" I asked.

Frank went from being a tough guy to a scared little boy. He looked at me with tears in his eyes.

"Trust me. This street life is harder than it looks, bro. Doing the right thing is much easier. Just think. If you were doing the right thing, then you would be having sweet dreams right now; instead you are out here, three digits away from spending ten years on lockdown. I can help you, man. If you let me," I said.

Frank took a deep breath and exhaled. He looked at me and dropped his head. "I'll be out here in the morning," he mumbled. "To get that trash up."

I nodded my head, and he walked off in the same direction as Kelli.

16

KWAME

I was left alone at the courts. Well, General Mack was with me, but not really. He was standing with his back toward me, staring out into the night, as still as a pole.

"General," I called.

No answer.

"General Mack," I called again, louder.

I walked over and stood directly in front of him. I leaned in for a closer look. This fool was asleep standing up. And had the nerve to be snoring.

I shook my head and sat on the park bench. I took another whiff of the thick ghetto air, then stood up. I decided I didn't want to spend my first night alone. I certainly didn't want to spend my first night of freedom out here waiting to see if General Mack was going to fall down and crack his head open. As entertaining as that may sound, I had a better idea.

I walked over to the apartment building where I remembered Kelli used to live with her mother. I hoped it was still the same one. I placed my ear to the door before knocking. I could hear the television on the other side. I decided to take a chance and tapped on the door.

Nothing.

I tapped again, this time a little louder, and a few seconds later the door swung open. Kelli stood there wearing a T-shirt and a pair of sleeping shorts that were threatening to burst at the seams.

Good Lord, I thought as I took in her track-star body.

"How you doing?" I asked.

She looked at me with a strange expression on her face. "I'm good. What's up?"

"I just wanted to talk to you," I said.

"Now?" She turned around and looked at the clock. "It's almost five in the morning."

"I know, but I don't like taking time for granted. Not even a second is promised to us," I said.

"Huh," she grunted.

"May I come in?" I asked.

She looked me up and down again before backing away from the door to allow me entry.

"Have a seat," she said. "I was up watching the news. I can't sleep anyway."

"Any good news to report?"

"Nope."

I almost forgot what it felt like to share company with a beautiful woman, and just the visual alone was like being in heaven.

"Are you hungry?" she asked.

Wow! I thought at the irony of those three words.

When I was incarcerated, I used to talk to a convict by the name of Julius "Jules" Jones. Jules had been locked up so long that he had forgotten what his crime was. Jules told me that when I was ready to find a wife, I would know I was on the right track when those three words were constantly coming out of her mouth.

When a woman wants to feed you, young blood, she's a good one. Are ya hungry? Those words let you know she's a caregiver and a woman of high character, Jules would say.

"Nah, my nana cooked enough food last night to hold me for a few weeks," I said, my eyes refusing to move from Kelli's shapely hips.

Kelli smiled and sat across from me on the love seat. "So, Mr. Braxton, what have you been up to?"

I took a deep breath. I wasn't prepared to answer that one. All of a sudden, I felt ashamed. I wanted to get up and walk out of her apartment, but I stayed put. Honesty was always the best policy, as Nana would say.

"I just got out of prison," I said, looking her straight in the eyes.

She winced and jerked her head back.

"And why were you in prison?" she asked calmly, as if incarceration was par for the course for young black men.

"For possession of narcotics with intent to distribute," I said, watching her every reaction.

"I see," she said. "Well, let me be honest with you, Kwame. I don't associate with drug dealers or ex-cons. I'm not judging you or anything, but I try to keep company with positive people."

"I'm not a drug dealer. I never sold drugs. I went to jail for that, but I didn't do it."

"That's a pretty typical response, Kwame, so pardon me if I seem like I don't believe you."

"That's fair, but there's nothing typical about me. I have a really good attorney who is appealing my sentence right now. I'm trying hard to clear my name. If I was guilty, I wouldn't be so concerned about that—after all, I've already done the time."

"Care to explain?" she said, crossing her legs Indian style and wrapping a blanket around her.

I sighed and thought carefully before I tried to explain to her how I went from being a college freshman to becoming state property.

July 15 was a day that changed my life forever. The sun was so hot it was threatening to burn a hole in my cranium as I walked along a huge curvy driveway with a weed eater. I had graduated from high school two weeks earlier and was due to leave for college in less than a month. I was trying to earn a few dollars so I could have some pocket money during my freshman year. One of my teachers owned a landscaping company and gave me a job cutting grass, bagging refuse, and planting flowers. I was hard at work when my cell phone rang with Wicked on the other end. He said he needed me to ride with him to pick up another car that he purchased from an auction off of Metropolitan Parkway. I agreed to help him and told my boss that I had to leave a little early.

"Man, I don't see how you work out here in that hot sun. You're already black as a field Negro," Wicked said as he picked me up. He was already deep into his street life, and try as I might, he wasn't hearing anything I had to say about getting a real job.

"The blacker the berry, the sweeter the juice, homie," I

said, climbing into the passenger seat of his plush Cadillac Escalade.

"I told you I can get you some real money. You won't have to do nothing but sit back and collect. Just like me. I sit in this big fine automobile and collect stacks."

"Yeah, and watch out for the cops."

"Nope," Wicked said with a gold-toothed smile. "They are on the payroll too."

"Yeah, okay. I think you've been watching too many movies, bro. But you'll see. This street thing never works out. Two years of getting paid for twenty years in the pen. Nah, I'll pass. Not the kind of life I'm tryna live, homie."

"Whatever. It beats being out here in the sun all day like some field hand. Singing slave songs to help the time pass."

"Yeah, well, if you keep on hustling, you'll see what a slave feels like soon enough. They still have chain gangs in Georgia, ya know."

"Stop putting that bad karma out there, boy."

We talked about my upcoming year at University of South Carolina and how I might get a few snaps at quarterback as a true freshman. Everyone said I was going to have to play wide receiver or return punts because they had a sophomore who was doing a phenomenal job at my same position. But my position coach called me with great news. The sophomore was a little homesick and was headed to a West Coast school so that he could be closer to home.

We made it to the auction and picked up the car. Wicked wanted to drive his new Benz, so I was left with the truck. I followed him out of the parking lot, and before I could make it fifty feet down Metropolitan, police

officers swarmed me from every direction. They surrounded the truck with guns drawn. My heart jumped out
of my chest as I saw my life flash before me. All I could do
was put my hands up.

"Get out of the car," they yelled, their guns trained on
me. "Move slowly."

I did as I was told.

The moment I was out of the truck, a cop sent his dog
into the vehicle and the canine was barking and scratching
at the backseat like there was no tomorrow.

"Jackpot," a cop said as he lifted the seat and removed
three big freezer-size bags of marijuana and a smaller bag
of what looked to me like chips of white soap.

Fear kicked into overdrive. I knew that wasn't soap in
that little bag—it was crack—and I was smart enough to
know that I was in some deep trouble.

I couldn't believe this was happening to me. I turned
my head and saw the black Mercedes that Wicked was driving had pulled into a hotel parking lot across the street.
He turned and looked right into my eyes. I could see the
conflict written all over his face. I could almost read his
thoughts.

*I don't want to leave my boy holding my bag, but if I
go over there, they are going to lock both of us up.*

Wicked made a rocking gesture with his hands and
shook his head. He was telling me he had to think about
his brand-new baby girl. Then he pulled off. My hands
were cuffed behind my back and I was shoved into the
back of a police car and my life was never the same.

"That favor cost me two years of my life, and I will never
get that time back for as long as I live," I said to Kelli.

"Why didn't you just tell the cops it wasn't your stuff?" Kelli asked innocently.

"I wish it was that easy. Much to my surprise, they had Wicked under surveillance for a minute. They had pictures and everything, so it wasn't like I could say I didn't know him. Two, you know how it is. You don't snitch. I guess I thought I was keeping it real by sticking to the code of the streets."

"So knowing what you know now, what would you do different?" she asked.

I smiled. That thought had played in my head every day for the last two years.

"I would sing like a bird. There is no code of the streets. Especially in our situation. I mean, if I was out there hustling like he's doing and I got caught, then, hey, you do the crime, you do your time—but that wasn't the case. And no friend is worth losing a part of your life like that. I've learned that friends come and go, and real friends wouldn't leave you hanging like that fool did. Also, if I had to do it over, I would've begged, borrowed, or stole to get a decent attorney. Half the guys in prison wouldn't be there if they had a good lawyer."

"And you guys are still friends after all that?"

"I wouldn't call us friends. Obviously that was never the case on his part, because a friend wouldn't let a friend do his time like that, but, hey, I don't blame him for what happened. I knew what he was about, but I still chose to hang out with him. I think he could've chipped in and got me an attorney, but I guess that would've been too much like the right thing to do."

Kelli nodded. I could see the wheels spinning in her head as she contemplated whether to believe my story.

"So what are your plans?" she asked.

"I don't know," I said, rubbing my temples. That was the question of the century for me. "I gotta do something, though."

Kelli stood and walked toward the kitchen. "Can I at least get you something to drink?"

"What do you have?"

"Orange juice, Kool-Aid, and water."

"What flavor Kool-Aid you got?"

"Red."

"I'll take the Kool-Aid," I said, smiling and wondering when red became a flavor.

Kelli brought me the drink and sat down beside me instead of on the love seat across from me. I took that as a sign that she didn't begrudge me my past.

"I'm not a bad person," I said.

"I know that and I'm sorry you had to go through what you did. Maybe God sent you there so you could save thousands of others from going. Who knows, maybe even millions."

"I appreciate you saying that. But I doubt God had anything to do with this. That place was hell, and we all know that's the Devil's playground. But I'm a guy who likes to let bygones be bygones. I don't dwell on negative things too much. Life is too short."

"Do you think you'll be able to talk to my nephew? Maybe talking to him about what you went through might help get his head on straight," Kelli asked.

"I can try, but he's a handful. I've seen his type a thousand times. Wannabe bad guys with no pedigree for the lifestyle. Video thugs."

"What's that?"

"Guys who watch videos all day long, studying how to be a thug," I said with a chuckle.

"He's dealing with a lot," Kelli said as sadness took over her face.

"Hanging out with Wicked is not the way to handle whatever he's dealing with, but I'll talk to him again."

"Thanks," Kelli said, looking up and smiling at me, then dropping her head. "I hurt so much for him. He lost his mother and his father in Hurricane Katrina."

All of a sudden, Spike Lee's movie popped in my head, and I visualized dead bodies floating in the streets. I felt sick, and every negative thought I had about young Franky disappeared.

"I'm sorry to hear that," I said.

"I almost died myself. Water was up to my neck, but then this nice old man riding around in a boat heard me screaming. He came over there and helped me. I don't even remember the ride—I guess I passed out. All I remember is waking up at the Superdome, thanking God that I was still alive," she said, wiping a tear away.

"I'm glad you're still here," I said, rubbing her back.

"And I'm glad you're back home." She smiled.

"So tell me about you. What's been going on in your life since the last time I saw you? Before the hurricanes, of course," I asked.

"Before the hurricanes, I was going to school, cheering and trying to finish up my tenth-grade year. I loved school so much. I was having the time of my life. Then the waters came," she said, and the tears came back. "I'm sorry."

"Don't be. It's okay," I said.

She cast her eyes on the floor and shook her head.

I stared at her. Man, she was fine. I wanted to touch her

so badly that I literally had to force myself to sit still. I don't know what it was, but I felt so connected to her. Our tragedies were very different, but they were tragedies nonetheless.

"I'm going to cook something because I'm starving. Are you sure you don't want anything?"

"Nah, I'm good," I said, picking up a novel she had lying on the coffee table.

A Killing in This Town, by Olympia Vernon.

"Is this a good book?" I called out.

"Yeah, I just cracked it open but so far so good. Are you a reader?"

"Yeah, that was mandatory in Nana's house. Not to mention where I was, a good book was like escaping for a few hours every day."

"Who's your favorite author?" she asked from the kitchen.

"Old school is Richard Wright. The new school, I like lots of people. Jihad, Eric Jerome Dickey, R. M. Johnson. I could go on and on."

"What do you think of all the street fiction books out now?"

"Some of the worst writing I've ever read, but who am I to judge? I don't know anyone's hustle. But it's not my cup of tea. How many times can you write about a drug dealer or a girl who's using a dude for his money? I like Shannon Holmes, though. He's good."

"I agree wholeheartedly. Never thought that books could be niggerized, but I guess I was wrong," she said, laughing.

I chuckled. I'd never heard the term *niggerized* before, but it seemed appropriate for a lot of what was going on today in the world.

I heard her humming; then she broke out into a full song. I put the book on the table and leaned back on the sofa. Here I was fresh out of prison, sitting on a raggedy sofa in the heart of the projects, but there was no place I'd rather be. I closed my eyes and enjoyed my own little neo-soul concert.

Just like that, I was in love. Not only was this woman beautiful, but she was also attentive, classy, and could sing with the best of them. I always said the woman I married would have to be fine, would have to sing, and would have to cook like my nana. What more could a man ask for?

17

ROMEO

*P*OW! *Pow! Pow! Pow! Pow! Pow!*
I jumped up in my bed at the familiar sound of gun-shots. It didn't matter how many times I heard those pops, I never got comfortable with them. I looked over at Kwame's bed and then at the clock. It was 10 a.m. He wasn't there, and my heart tried to pound itself out of my chest. I threw my legs over the edge of my bed and ran from our room wearing only my boxer underwear. I peeked into the bathroom before walking into the kitchen, but he wasn't there either.

"Nana, where's Kwame?" I asked.

"I don't know. He left outta here about three o'clock this morning. I haven't seen him since," she said with a worried look on her face.

I ran back to my room and threw on a pair of shorts and slipped my feet into my Nike flip-flops. I turned right back around and ran from the apartment bare-chested.

I ran through the breezeway just before I heard more

shots. I turned to my left to see our neighbor Mr. Harold pointing his gun in the air for another round of shots.

Pow! Pow! Pow!

"Mr. Harold, what are you doing out here shooting your gun like that?" I asked.

"Just letting them fools know it's up in here," he said just as he squeezed off a few more.

Mr. Harold lived in a house behind our projects. The fence people hadn't completed the job yet, so I could still walk directly out of the apartment and into his yard. He was a widower and an overall nice guy, but he could get rowdy with the best of them once he started drinking.

"Have you seen my brother?"

"Some little punks robbed me last night. I went to play bingo and I came home and these lil bad bastards done been in my home," he said, reloading his pistol. "So, since they wanna see what's in my home, I'ma let them know what's really up in here."

"I'm sorry to hear that, Mr. Harold," I said.

"Yeah, them lil bums who robbed me gonna be sorry, too, when I find out who did it. You know I'ma find them, too, don't you?"

"I'm sure you will, Mr. Harold."

"What 'bout that you asked me, Romeo?"

"Have you seen my brother?" I asked again.

"Kwame? He out?"

I guess that answered my question.

"Yeah, he's out, but Nana said he left early this morning and didn't come home."

"Probably nothing to worry about, baby boy. Man's been away for a few years. He's probably out there getting some of that pressure off him. If you know what I mean."

"A'ight, Mr. Harold. I'll talk to you later."

"Hey," he called out. "Tell Beatrice I said . . ." Mr. Harold cocked his lip up and gave an overexaggerated wink of his eye. His message to my nana. He loved her dirty bloomers, but she paid him no attention. The only time she would say more than one word to him was when there was a bump in the night. The first thing she would do at the slightest sound was reach for the phone and ask Mr. Harold to come over. And he was always anxious to oblige, as he would storm into our place with his mini arsenal.

"I'll make sure I tell her," I said.

I walked around to Amir's house to see if he had seen my brother, but I caught him on the way out. He was pushing his mother's wheelchair down onto the sidewalk.

"Good morning, Miss Jackson. Where you headed off to so early this morning?" I said.

"Boy, it's eleven o'clock. Ain't nothing early about eleven o'clock," she said.

"Why can't you ever answer a question without all the extras?"

"Because I'm grown and I can do whatever I feel like doing," she said, fanning me off. "Don't you get smart with me, Romeo. I'll get up outta this chair and knock the black off of you."

I turned to Amir. "What's up, boy? Have you seen Kwame?"

"He's home?"

"Yeah," I said, turning to scan the projects. "Where y'all headed off to?"

"Going to the doctor's office. Somebody's been having chest pains and not telling me."

"Oh, cut it out. Ain't nothing wrong with me," Miss Jackson said. "Amir, you get on my nerves sometimes. You worry more than an old lady."

"Romeo, you going to work today?" Amir asked.

"Yeah, I'm going."

"Well, tell somebody I'ma be late," Amir said.

"You're always late. I don't even need to tell nobody that."

"Tell them anyway."

"Bye, Miss Jackson," I said, walking off. "I gotta go and see if I can find my brother."

"Romeo," she called out. "Tell Kwame I said come by and see me. I'd love to see his old knotty-head self."

"I'll tell him," I said with a sinking feeling that something wasn't right.

I walked toward the basketball courts, because someone was always there to give you lowdowns of the projects, but before I could make it over there, I saw General Mack. He was kneeling down over what appeared to be a body.

"General, what are you doing?" I asked.

"Call a medic, soldier," he screamed at the top of his lungs.

I shook my head and calmly walked over to him. I looked down and saw that somebody had gotten a pretty bad beat-down. Upon further inspection, I could see the blood-covered face belonged to a woman. I looked a little closer and did a double take. My eyes bulged out with surprise when I recognized the face of my mother.

18

ROMEO

I ran to the first door I could get to and banged on it as hard as I could.

"Help!" I screamed, still banging. "Hey, open the door. I need some help."

No answer.

I ran to a different door and banged again. This time the door flew open and Mark, Wicked's skinny little flunky, was standing there with his bony chest out and a pair of jeans hanging so low on his waist that they were barely covering his private parts.

"What the hell you want?" he said, chewing something that resembled a chicken wing.

"Call nine-one-one. My mom needs some help," I said frantically.

"What's it worth to you, punk?" He smiled, obviously unaware of the graveness of my mother's situation.

I didn't have time to explain it to him. I reared back and punched him in the face as hard as I could. He went down like a sack of potatoes. I raced past him and picked up the phone that was sitting on a table by the sofa.

No dial tone.

"Aughhh!" I yelled, looking around.

That vicious-looking pit bull was in a doggy kennel chewing at the handle, no doubt trying to escape so that he could take a bite out of me. I looked around and saw that Mark had a cell phone hanging from his hip. I ran over to him, reached down, and snatched it up. He grabbed my leg, and I punched him on the top of his head with a right that would've staggered Mike Tyson. He released his grip and passed out.

I flipped open the phone and dialed 911. I asked the operator for an ambulance. Whoever was on the line got on my nerves, acting as if they had all day.

"May I have your location?" she asked.

"The Village Apartments."

"What is your name?"

"Why?"

"Do you have a call-back number?"

"No."

"Can you tell me what the victim is wearing?"

"Man, will you get somebody over here? She'll be the one lying on the ground with blood all over her clothes," I said before hanging up the phone.

I threw the phone back at Mark, who was still lying stiff as a board. I grabbed the forty-ounce bottle of beer that was sitting on the table in front of the television and poured it on him. The liquid helped his recovery, and he shook his head to clear the cobwebs. I stepped over him and ran back outside, heading straight for Nana.

"Nana!" I screamed as I burst through the door.

"What's the matter?" she asked, no doubt expecting some bad news about Kwame.

"It's Pearl. Somebody beat her up and the ambulance is on the way," I said, pulling her by her arm toward the door. "Come on. She's down there with General Mack bleeding all over the place."

"Oh, Lord." Nana pulled away from me with a frustrated look on her face. She walked over and sat on the sofa.

"Come on, Nana," I said, wondering why she was so uninterested in the well-being of her daughter.

She held up a hand to me and closed her eyes. She seemed to be praying. When she opened her eyes, she turned to me.

"You put on some clothes and go," she said. "I can't deal with Pearl right now."

Something about the look on my grandmother's face wouldn't allow me to question her. I went to my room and changed into a pair of sweats and some tennis shoes. I walked back out and placed a hand on my grandmother's shoulder, giving her a gentle squeeze. She didn't deserve to deal with this drama so close to the joy of Kwame coming home.

Where in the heck is he, anyway?

"I'll let you know what's going on with her. Are you okay?" I asked.

She nodded, but I could tell she wasn't in the mood for words. I walked out of the door.

I made my way back to the spot where Pearl was already being lifted into the back of an ambulance.

"Is she going to be okay?" I asked the paramedic.

"Not sure. Who are you?" asked the guy in the blue shirt with a medical patch on his chest pocket.

"I'm her son."

"Hop in," he said, pointing to the open doors of the vehicle.

I rode in the back of the ambulance as the medical guys worked on Pearl. Even though we weren't close, I felt something vile growing in me as I looked at the pain someone had inflicted on my mother. The paramedics asked me question after question about her medical history, but I wasn't much help to them. I realized then how little I really knew about my mother.

When we arrived at DeKalb Medical Center, they rushed her into the emergency room. I was left to pace the halls and try to figure out my next move. I didn't feel much of anything. No worry, no fear, no love. I felt guilty for my lack of emotions, but that's the hand we were dealt.

What if she dies? I wondered. How would I feel about that? How would Nana or Kwame feel about losing her?

I shook off the peculiar thoughts running through my mind, because to me, she had been dead for ten years. But I wondered why she was reaching out to me all of a sudden?

Why was she at my game?

What was really going on with her?

All of these questions rumbled around in my mind.

"What's up, man?" Kwame said, rushing up to me in the hallway of the hospital.

"Where you been?" I snapped.

"At a friend's. What's going on?" he said calmly.

"I don't know. I went looking for you and saw General Mack tryna give her CPR. Looks like somebody beat her up pretty bad."

Kwame frowned but didn't say anything.

"What friend are you talking about?" I asked, not letting go of his whereabouts.

Kwame pushed past me without answering. He walked up to the nurses' station and spoke to the lady sitting behind the desk.

"Rome," Kwame called after a few seconds of speaking with the lady. "Come on."

We followed the nurse back to a curtained-off section where our mother was lying. It seemed as though every part of her body had been hit. She looked over at us and forced a smile.

"My babies," she said, just above a whisper.

"Hey, Pearl," I said. "What happened to you?"

She fanned me away and tried to act as if her beat-down was no big deal.

"I'm so happy to see y'all," she said, still whispering. "Oh, Kwame, you look so much like your daddy."

"Mom," Kwame spoke up. He always called her Mom no matter what had transpired in the past. "What's happened to you? Who did this?"

She turned away, shaking her head. Then she closed her eyes and drifted off to sleep. The medication had taken effect and our questions would have to wait.

A tall white lady, who appeared to be in her late fifties, came through the entryway to the curtain. Kwame and I turned toward her.

"Are you guys her sons?" she said, walking over to

where we were standing. She quickly covered her mouth with her diamond-studded hand when she saw Pearl's condition.

"Yeah—" I started.

"Who are you?" Kwame said, holding up a hand to quiet me.

"My name is Joyce Marina, and I'm a friend of your mother," she said, staring down at our mother with genuine hurt in her eyes.

"What kind of friend?" Kwame asked. "And how did you know she was here?"

"Your grandmother told me," she said.

"Rome, have you ever seen this lady before?"

"Nope," I said. But I wasn't sure why Kwame was giving her the rough treatment.

She seemed caught off guard, as if she didn't understand why she was getting the third degree.

"Your mother works for me. When she didn't show up for work today, I went to the address she gave me and your grandmother said she was here."

"You do this for all of your employees who don't show up for work?" Kwame asked.

"No, but I consider your mother a friend. And she's special because, well . . . She's just special to me. So I felt a need to check up on her," she said, obviously tiring of the inquisition.

"Somebody assaulted my mother. Do you know anyone who would want to hurt her?" Kwame asked.

Mrs. Marina placed a hand over her mouth and dropped her head. "I don't know who would try to hurt her. God, I hope she didn't go and do something foolish."

"What do you mean? And what kind of work was my mother doing for you?" Kwame asked.

She hunched her shoulders. "Little cleaning projects around the facility."

"What facility?" I asked.

"I run a health center called ReEnter. Pearl has been with me off and on for the last ten years, and lately she has been working really hard to get her life back on track."

"Did anything seem out of the ordinary lately?" Kwame asked.

"She was on the phone a lot. And I would hear her shouting, but when I came in the room, she would hang up. I could overhear her saying something about how she was going to the papers or the news station or something like that, but when I asked her about it, she wouldn't give me any answers. She did this for the last few days. A few days ago, she had a visitor. In all the time Pearl has been with me, the only visitor she's ever had has been her mother."

"Who was the visitor?" I asked.

"Not sure. But Pearl went with him, and when she returned, she seemed happy."

Kwame walked over to Mrs. Marina. "So do you have anything on the visitor? I need to know everything you know about this person my mother has been hanging around."

"I don't know much. Just that he dropped her off and picked her up, but something about him seemed up to no good to me. *Shady* is a good word to describe him."

"What kind of car did he drive?" Kwame asked.

"One of those big military-looking vehicles."

"A Hummer," I said.

"I don't know. It was a big square-looking thing. One of those sports-utility things. It was white. And it had those shiny wheels. That's all I know."

Kwame extended his hand. "I'm sorry about the way I treated you earlier. It's just we can't be too careful now that someone is out there trying to hurt our mother."

Mrs. Marina shook his hand and nodded that she understood.

"As you probably know, my mother has been on drugs for a while, but she's still my mom and I'm not going to let anybody use her as a punching bag," Kwame said.

Mrs. Marina nodded. "How old are you?" she asked Kwame.

"I'm nineteen."

"And you?" she said, turning to me.

"I'm seventeen."

"I see. Well, like I said, I've known your mother for about ten years, and I've never known her to use drugs," she said.

Kwame looked at me and I returned his confused look.

"Well, what do you call what she uses?" I asked.

Mrs. Marina seemed temporarily at a loss for words, then said, "She's not on any form of illegal narcotic. And we test our employees regularly. No one is exempt. Not even me. We've never had a problem with Pearl and drugs."

"Well, what's wrong with her?" I asked.

"Oh, my," she said. "You don't know, do you?"

"Know what?" Kwame snapped.

"I don't know if I should be the one to tell you," she said.

"Mrs. Marina, we're not little boys anymore. Somebody wanted to hurt my mom. This isn't some random act of violence. People in our neighborhood know who she is, so they're not gonna lay a finger on her. Now, from what you say, she may be mixed up with some shady people. I need to know what's going on," Kwame said.

Mrs. Marina shifted a little in place. She looked around the room until her eyes focused on Pearl.

"Your mother suffers from schizoaffective disorder, which is something of a cross between bipolar disorder and schizophrenia. When she takes her medication, she does well. When she doesn't, she can get violent, and it's easy to confuse what she suffers from with the characteristics of a drug addict. But trust me, your mother's no addict."

"He's a liar and I'ma make him pay. Dirty Harry," Pearl said, waking up and looking around. But just as suddenly as she popped up, she was back off to sleep before we could get a question in.

"That's normal. You won't get much out of her right now. She's heavily medicated." Mrs. Marina reached in her purse and removed a business card. "Please call me if you need anything."

Kwame took the card and shook her hand again. I walked over and did the same.

Mrs. Marina walked over to our mother and leaned down to rub her forehead with her pale white hand. She stood, wiped away a tear, and rushed from the room.

"I'll be right back," Kwame said, leaving the room.

I walked over to Pearl and felt really bad for her. Why did things have to be like this? Seeing her in this condition and hearing that drugs were never her issue made me blame her for nothing and forgive her for everything.

I rubbed the top of her hand with mine and told her to hang in there.

19

ROMEO

I looked up from my mother's bed and saw Ngiai standing in the hospital doorway looking at me. Her flawless skin, silky long hair, and bright eyes immediately lit up the room. "Hey," she said, walking over to me. "Is she going to be okay?"

"Don't know yet. How did you know I was here?"

"Nana told me. I called your cell phone, but obviously you didn't have it with you," she said, handing me my phone. "Nana said to call her as soon as you can."

"Thanks," I said, taking the phone and turning it on. "I'm surprised to see you. I thought you didn't want anything to do with me."

"I never said that. I remember saying we would always be friends," Ngiai said, walking over to my mother. She straightened out Pearl's hair with her hand. She rubbed it down and showed the gentleness I've always known her to have. "What happened to her?"

"Somebody beat her up," I said, and the thought sent a sickening feeling through me.

"Who would do a thing like that?" she said with a frown.

"I don't know," I said. "Some cowards."

A doctor came in the area and said we had to leave while he took Pearl to get some type of medical attention. I surprised myself by leaning down and kissing my mother on the forehead.

"Thanks for coming," I said once we were out in the hallway and walking to the waiting area.

"No problem," she said. "Why haven't you called me?"

"You told me you needed your space and that it was over," I said.

"Yeah, but I expected you to call me or something. Check up on me or something."

"I was just tryna be respectful of your wishes," I said.

"Were you, or is it that you just don't care?"

"I care. Why would you say that?"

"I think this is the first time since we've been together that I went that long without talking to you. It's been over a week, Romeo."

I sighed and hunched my shoulders. My mind wasn't on this situation because my mom had all of my attention.

Ngiai must've read my thoughts. She looked at me, then turned to leave. "Give your mother my best," she said.

"Wait a minute," I said, snapping out of it. I felt compelled to say something. I missed my girl, and I wasn't about to let her just walk out like that. "I missed you."

"What do you miss? I wasn't giving you anything," she said sarcastically.

"Come on, man, don't do that," I said, shaking my head. "I'm sorry. What can I do to make things right between us?"

She looked at me hard and long. Tears streamed down her face. I hated when she cried.

"I can't believe you did that. I thought we were better than that. I mean, this is me. Us. Me and you. I thought we were bigger than that."

"We are. It's just . . . I . . . ," I said, then stopped myself from making excuses. "I'm sorry."

"I feel like a fool. It was one thing for me to deal with the rumors. I could always chalk that up to the haters, but for it to be real? That hurt. That really hurt, Romeo."

"Can we get out of here? Can we take a ride and talk?"

"What about your mom?"

"Kwame's here. He can handle it. Let me just run and tell him we're leaving," I said, reading her eyes to see if I was asking too much.

"Go ahead," she said.

I hustled over to the nurses' station and asked the lady if she had seen my brother, but before she could respond, I saw him walking down the hall.

"Ngiai's here and we're gonna get out of here for a few. We need to talk about that thing I was telling you about."

"Go ahead," he said. "I just called Nana. She didn't sound so good, so make sure you stop by there and check up on her. I'm gonna stay up here for a while."

"Hi, Kwame," Ngiai said with a smile.

"Hey there, baby girl," Kwame said, walking over to her and giving her a hug.

"You think you have enough muscles?" Ngiai said, touching his arm.

Kwame smiled and fanned her off. "You guys be careful out there," he said.

"Will do," I said, and we hugged before I walked out to deal with another saga.

20

ROMEO

"So where do you want to go?" Ngiai said, buckling herself into the driver's seat of her car.

"It doesn't matter. Any place other than here."

"Okay," she said, easing out of the parking lot and into the busy street. "I'm sorry to hear about your mom."

"Thanks. I just found out that she was never on drugs. She has mental problems. I don't know which one is worse."

Ngiai frowned and looked at me as if I should know better. "You should be happy to hear that."

"Why?"

"Because one is a choice—the other is not," she said. "Did you know that black people are the least likely of all races to seek help for mental problems?"

"I bet."

"And it's stupid because if you have cancer, you'll go get help, but if you have mental problems, there's a negative stigma. That's crazy. Who made that rule up?"

"I guess you're right. It's just we always look at people with mental problems as if they are weird."

"Yes, but we shouldn't. We think we can pray our way out of anything. God placed doctors here on Earth for a reason. Do you feel like going out to my house?"

"That's cool," I said, and turned to stare out of the passenger window as we left the busy downtown section of Decatur and headed out to the quietness of Fayetteville, Georgia, where the black folks lived like kings and queens.

I always enjoyed visiting Fayetteville. To me there was nothing better than being around people who looked just like you and were doing well for themselves. Million-dollar homes were in abundance, and seeing a guy in his early twenties or sometimes younger driving a Bentley or a Range Rover that was paid for with legitimate funds wasn't out of the norm. I made a pact with myself to put Nana in one of those big, beautiful houses the minute I made some real money.

"Why are you so quiet?" Ngiai asked.

"Just thinking. Got a lot on my mind, I guess," I said.

She nodded.

"I miss you, though," I said.

She nodded again but said nothing.

"I don't know what I was thinking. I guess I wasn't thinking," I said.

"Was that the first time you cheated on me?"

"Yeah," I answered honestly. I had had more than my share of opportunities to get busy with a number of girls, but my love for Ngiai always overruled my lustful desires.

"You know I don't believe you, right?"

I hunched my shoulders. "I guess I can't blame you, but I'm telling the truth."

We turned into her subdivision and had to stop in the middle of the street while a dozen or so ducks took their time crossing the road.

Ngiai's house was at the end of a cul-de-sac. It was an awesome combination of white bricks and tan shutters. The house sat on an acre and a half of manicured landscaping. It boasted a four-car garage, a swimming pool with a beautiful waterfall as a backdrop, and a tennis court that also served as a full-sized basketball court. Those were just a few of the bells and whistles that made the house the baddest boy on the block.

Standing between two twelve-foot wrought-iron doors was Beau Harris, Ngiai's stepdad.

Beau was as clean-cut as you could get. But there was something underneath the surface of his Tiger Woods–like persona (the one he had before the sex scandal) that said he would go tooth and nail to protect the existence he'd carved out in this crazy world.

Beau always told me the only thing he hated more than self-destructive blacks was black people who looked down on the have-nots.

"Looka here," he said, walking down the steps toward us. He opened Ngiai's door and held it while she got out. "Your mother is on the way to the mall. Better catch her while you can," he said.

Ngiai smiled at the mere mention of shopping. She jumped out of the car and hustled toward the house without so much as looking back at me.

"Hey! Wait a minute. I can't be out here all day. I know how you get in those malls," I said. "You know I gotta get back to my side of town."

"I'll get you home," Beau said.

Ngiai waved at me and ran around the side of the house to catch up with her mother, who was already backing out of the driveway. She jumped into the car and buckled up.

"Hey, Romeo," Mrs. Harris, Ngiai's mom, called out to me through the window of her Jaguar. "You know I'm gonna spank your little butt, don't you?"

I tilted my head as I walked toward her, asking for forgiveness with my eyes.

"Aww, pick your head up," she said, still backing down the driveway. She tossed her hand out in a wave, and they were on their way.

"Come on in, man," Beau said, turning to walk back through the front door.

I followed him inside and once again was amazed at the way some people lived. His house was the same size as the entire building I lived in. I had been in this house a hundred times, but each time I was more impressed than I was the time before. The foyer was a huge oasis of marble and stone. Hand-carved art pieces adorned the walls. Leather and suede furniture gave the house a homey and welcoming feel.

We went into the house's study, which was right off the stone and marble foyer. Beau took a seat behind the massive desk that was hand-carved in some foreign country, and pointed at a leather chair.

"Have a seat," he said the minute he sat down. "You want something to drink?"

"No, thanks," I said before easing down into the chair. I looked around the walls that were lined with books and pictures of him in his former life as a professional baseball player.

I still remember the first time I met him. We were all

running around playing in the hood, and this big, fancy car pulled up and this light-skinned man with curly hair stepped out and walked over to us.

"Which one of you boys goes by the name of Romeo?"

I was hesitant at first, but then he smiled.

"Me."

"You got a thing for Ngiai?"

All of the other kids started chiding me and hooping and hollering about me getting beat up.

"She's my friend."

"Well, I'm going to marry her mother, which is going to make her my daughter. Now, if you wanna be in my good graces, you'll treat her good. Is that a deal?"

"Deal," I said, shaking his hand.

We have been cool ever since.

"First of all, I'm not mad at you. You guys shouldn't be so serious about each other, anyway, especially at this age. But at the same time, I was your age before and I know how it feels to think you're in love."

I smiled and nodded. If what I felt for Ngiai wasn't love, then I didn't want to experience real love, because my every waking moment was all about her.

"What's going on with you right now, Romeo, is called life. And, brother-man, there's a reason it's a four-letter word. The good thing is, you didn't get *my* daughter pregnant. The bad part of it is, you got *somebody's* daughter pregnant, and being that you are just a baby yourself, that makes things complicated."

"I'm not a baby, man," I protested.

"Yes, you are. In the grand scheme of life, Romeo, you don't know a thing. What can you offer a child right now? You're seventeen years old and you live with your grandmother. And I'm not knocking you for that. You are right where you're supposed to be at this point in your life."

I started feeling a little dressed down because he was right.

"Do you know why Ngiai won't have sex with you? Because I told her not to, and she trusts me. She trusts that I have her best interest at heart, and she believes that I won't lead her wrong. You guys have the rest of y'all lives to go and screw like rabbits, but right now . . ." He shook his head. "Nah, these are the building years, youngster. Life is like a house—if you take the time to build a solid foundation, then the rest is gravy, but if you mess around and build a shabby foundation, then you'll forever have problems with it. You'll spend all of your time trying to fix what you halfway did in the first place, and eventually you'll have to tear it down and start from scratch. At your age, Romeo, one bad choice can affect you for the rest of your life. And you will see that when this baby arrives."

"I'll be okay. I'm not some deadbeat, and I'm not even sure that girl is telling the truth," I said.

"Well, time will fix that one too. But you gotta think," Beau said, pointing to his head, "this girl you got knocked up, is she the type of woman you want to have to deal with for the rest of your life?"

"Nah," I said, thinking about how hood and ghetto fabulous Vonetta was.

Beau shook his head and chuckled. "But that's exactly what position you put yourself in. See, Romeo, you're hot stuff right now, and I'm sure all the little girls are crazy about you, but forget all that. You can never get too caught up in the moment. I can't count the number of guys I knew who were hot stuff in high school. I see them now and they're out on the street begging for cigarettes. And they are there because of that sorry foundation they built for themselves."

"I know a dude with a PhD who sleeps under the bridge over by our building," I said.

"Okay . . . ?"

"I'm sure he had a solid foundation," I said.

"Romeo, nothing is absolute. What I'm saying doesn't apply to all people, just most. I'm not sure what bricks were thrown at the man with the PhD who sleeps under the bridge."

"That's not gonna be me," I said adamantly.

"I hope not. But you gotta plan your life like you plan to live it for a while. And as far as schools go, colleges these days aren't just looking for athletes. Skills alone ain't gonna cut it. They want the total package. It's about character, and these high-level programs don't want guys without it. They are looking hard for these future 'Mr. Make It Rain' so they can stay away from him."

"So you saying I don't have character just because I made a mistake?"

"No, I know you have tons of character because I know you personally. But what you have to understand is that these college coaches don't know you from a hole in the wall. Here's what they see when they look at you. An outstanding athlete for one. But then they see you as a project boy who has a brother who was also an outstanding athlete but who somehow landed in prison."

"He's out," I corrected.

"Okay, they see an ex-con for a brother who was just as

talented and ended up in jail on some drug nonsense.
They see a baby on the way, and all that adds up to a problem. You seem careless to them."

"So what do I do, Beau? Pack it in and get a job at
Kroger?"

"Nah, you flip it. You make it work for you. You don't
shy away from your responsibility—you hit it head-on. You
own up to it and don't call it a mistake."

"I just hate that I messed it up with Ngiai."

"Ngiai will be fine. She's strong and very understanding
for her age. You decided on a school yet?"

"Nah."

"Can I make a suggestion?"

"I already know. Go far away."

"Nah, just the opposite. Georgia Tech has a great program, and UGA isn't bad either. Even Georgia State is on
the come up."

"Yeah, I wanna stay close by. Just heard some news
about my mom that makes me want to stay close to
home."

"Ngiai told me about your mother, and I'm sorry to
hear about that. Pardon me for not mentioning it earlier,"
Beau said with concern in his eyes. "Is she going to be
okay?"

"I don't know. We'll see. I found out that she was never
on drugs. She has mental problems."

Beau nodded and rubbed his chin. "Well, if there's anything I can do to help you guys with that, don't hesitate to
call on me."

"I appreciate that," I said, ready to get off that subject.
"You know I love The A, and I can't see myself going too
far away from it."

"Be careful with that one, Romeo. Now, I know you got your little friends, but you need to separate yourself from guys who aren't on your level. And whether you want to acknowledge it or not, you are on a different level, young man. You need to recognize those who aren't going where you are and make sure you stay clear of them. Never be afraid to admit that you are better than someone. Your brother was better than the guy he was hanging with when he got into that trouble. He paid the price for dumbing down. Can you imagine LeBron James hanging out with some little ignorant clown on the street and getting locked up for so-called keeping it real? The world would've missed out on a phenomenal athlete, and he would've tossed away a great life for himself, not to mention hundreds of millions of dollars. But as crazy as it sounds, young people do it every day. All in the name of 'keeping it real.' Black people's favorite saying is, 'don't forget where you come from.' Well, damn that. If remembering where I come from means letting you leach off of me, then I'm getting a quick case of amnesia."

I chuckled. Beau always gave me a different line of reasoning.

"But I don't want to forget where I come from and turn into some nerd living in a bubble."

"I'm not saying forget who you are, and you should always appreciate where you come from, but never embrace it. When you embrace something, you don't want to let it go. And ghetto life is something that should be released the first opportunity you have."

"So how can I let it go if I stay home to go to college?"

"Easy. Speak to the clowns and keep it moving. As a matter of fact, you owe it to them to better yourself. And they need to see it happen. I'm from here. I grew up right over there in College Park. My daddy was a self-made man. He got up every morning and put the work in. And when my uncles, who were drunks and womanizers, tried to come and live with us when they fell on hard times, Pops always said no."

"Why wouldn't he help his own brothers out?" I asked. "He didn't have any love for them?"

"It wasn't that he didn't love his brothers, but he knew that he lived the life he deserved by working hard, and they didn't deserve the same thing, because they were lazy and always took shortcuts. My uncles worked hard at having fun. Drinking and partying their lives away wasn't going to do it. No way they should share the same lifestyle as a man who worked seventy maybe eighty hours a week."

My cell phone rang. It was Kwame. He told me to make my way back to the hospital, because Pearl was up and she was asking for me.

"Beau, thanks for the talk, man. I really appreciate it, but that was my brother and he said I need to make my way back to DeKalb Medical Center."

"Let's go," he said.

21

ROMEO

We hurried outside, where Beau had a fleet of exotic automobiles. He walked over to the black Porsche 911, so I hopped in the passenger side. He chatted about life some more, but my mind was on my mother and how badly I'd treated her in the past.

We arrived at the hospital in less than a half hour.

"Do you need me to stay?" Beau asked.

"Nah, but thanks for the ride, man, and the talk," I said, reaching over to shake his hand.

"If you need me, call me. And, Romeo," Beau said, leaning over the passenger seat, "keep your head up. You're a good kid."

"Thanks, Beau," I said, getting out of the car.

I hustled into the hospital and sprinted through the hallways, following the signs that led me to the emergency room. All of a sudden, I felt a sense of urgency to get to Pearl.

Kwame was standing in the hallway with his hands behind his back. When he saw me, his face lit up.

"What's up, man?" I said, walking up to him and shaking his hand.

"She's asleep now, but I'm sure when she wakes up again, she'll be calling for you."

"Did you talk to Nana?"

"Nah. Did you get a chance to go by there?" he asked.

"No, we went out to Ngiai's house."

There was a loud voice in the distance. Then there was a high-pitched voice arguing with the first one. I turned my head and noticed General Mack marching down the hallway with a security guard right on his tail. Kwame and I must've been thinking the same thing, because we started walking toward him.

"He's okay," Kwame said to the security guard.

"No, he's not okay. He has to leave right now," the old security guard with the soprano voice said.

"At ease, soldier," the general barked at the guard. "Top-secret priority meeting going on here. Back up, private."

"Private? I'm a sergeant and you gonna leave my hospital," the guard shot back.

"Yo hospital! Niggaro, please. You need to check yourself into one of these rooms 'cause you suffering from a big fat case of delusions of grandeur. Yo three-dollar-an-hour booty can't even spell *hospital*. Where your firearm at?"

"I don't need a firearm for the likes of you." The old man stepped back into a fighting stance.

"General, what are you doing here?" Kwame asked, coming between the two senior citizens who were about to kill each other.

"Came to bring yo nana up here. I escorted her on the MARTA train. Made sure she got here safe."

"Where is she?"

"Down the hall taking care of some paperwork. Now I need to have a Joint Chiefs of Staff meeting outside. Away from . . ." The general nodded at the old security guard.

"Yeah, get outside," the security guard said, huffing and puffing. "And don't come back."

"At ease, soldier," the general barked. "I'll take care of you later."

The general did his crooked about-face and stomped away as if he was in the Communist army.

We walked out of a side door, and the general came straight at me. He stopped about two inches away from my face, and I almost died from funk inhalation. Eewww! The general's breath smelled like a dead dog.

"Didn't I tell you to check it out? Those the same folks I saw drop yo momma off. Now! Now will you do what I asked you to do, soldier?" he snapped.

"What folks?" I asked.

"Hell if I know. All I know is I know the enemy when I smell him. And I was right on target as usual," he said, finally backing away and giving my nostrils a welcome reprieve.

"Who dropped our mom off, General?" Kwame asked calmly.

"Two white boys. Well, one white boy and a high-yellow fella. Driving a military vehicle. Humvee type. Color white. Big shiny wheels on it. Looked like crap."

Kwame and I looked at each other. That was the same kind of car Mrs. Marina had mentioned seeing.

"I got a plate number. You add that to the address I

gave your forgetful brother and we might be cooking with grease," General said, handing the slip of paper to Kwame this time.

"What address?" Kwame asked.

"It was an envelope. It fell out of their truck, and I gave it to that one there to do his research," he said, pointing at me. "Had some good info on it."

"Let's go," I said.

Neither Kwame nor the general took a step. I stopped and looked back. "Come on, man, let's go."

"Let's go where? Where are you going?" Kwame asked.

"To get that envelope. We gotta get at these fools, Kwame. They can't just come around beating up on Pearl like that," I said.

"Calm down," Kwame said. "We'll get them, but this isn't a street fight. When we go at these guys, we'll have to be prepared. And besides, you're gonna stay outta this. I'll handle it."

"You crazy. That's my mom, too, and I'm not some little boy who you can send in the house when things get hot," I snapped.

"No. You're crazy if you think for one second I'm about to let you get caught up in this mess. Now, I said I'll handle it, and that's what I'm gonna do," Kwame said, getting in my face, daring me to say another word.

AWWWW, man, I thought.

He could always beat me in a fistfight. Not that we ever really had one, but when we wrestled, I never stood a chance. And with all the muscles he built up in prison, I didn't see how anything had changed on that front.

"Romeo, I believe your brother's right," General said. "Why don't you sit this one out, soldier?"

"Man, forget that. I'm not some—" I said, but before I could say another word, I was slapped and Kwame's large hand wrapped its way around my neck and slammed me against the wall.

"You're gonna go in there and sit in the waiting room until Mom wakes up. And once she wakes up, you're going to sit your little butt down and keep her company. That's what you're gonna do, Romeo. But you will leave this thing alone and let me handle it. Do you understand?"

I didn't say anything. Actually, I couldn't say anything. My vocal cords were a little tied up. Tears were starting to stream down my face. Not because I was hurt, but because I couldn't breathe.

He released his grip, and all I could do was double over in pain and gasp for air.

"Man," I said, still holding on to my neck. "What's wrong with you?"

Kwame gave me a look that I had never seen before. I decided right then and there to leave his crazy butt alone. I didn't want to push my luck with his newfound aggression.

"Where did you put the address?" he asked.

"In my jeans," I said.

"Where are they?"

"I don't know. You said you were going to handle it. So you figure it out," I said, and turned around and walked back inside the hospital. I made my way down the busy corridor.

I sat in the cold waiting room, looking at other people

who were there for their loved ones. I got restless after
about twenty minutes of doing nothing. I flipped open my
cell phone and dialed Ngiai's number. I missed my girl,
and with all the drama that was going on, I really could
use a friendly voice, but my call went straight to her voice
mail. I hung up without leaving a message. Just as I
flipped my phone closed, it rang. I looked at the screen
and saw it was Amir.

"What's up, bro?" I said.

"What happened?" he asked, skipping the formalities.

"I don't know. Somebody beat my mom up."

"What the . . . ? Where you at?"

"DeKalb Medical Center."

"You want me to come down there?"

"Nah, man. I'm good. All I'm doing is sitting in the waiting room anyway. They won't let me in to see her."

"Man, that's jacked up. I just saw a couple of police officers leaving your apartment. The door was open and it
looks like somebody went in there and tore the place up."

"What?" I said, standing up. "They went into our apartment?"

"Yeah, man. Somebody went in there. What's going
on?"

"I don't know," I said as I walked out into the hallway. I
saw a few doctors talking to Nana. I ducked back so she
wouldn't see me. "I'm on my way. I'll see you in a few."

22

ROMEO

I jumped on the bus at the corner of Church Street and North Decatur Road. I sat in the front of the bus as usual and smiled when I thought of where I had picked up that habit. My mother sat me and Kwame down and made us watch any and everything related to the civil rights movement. She told us that some black people were so conditioned to being second-class citizens that they found a way to make it cool.

"Watch some black folks when they get on the bus. They will go straight to the back," she would say. *"Make sure y'all always sit up front. And that goes for anyplace. Well, except the movie theater—sit in the middle,"* she would say, then smile.

Now that I knew my mother wasn't on drugs, it was amazing how differently I looked at her. As I rode the bus the short distance back to our apartments, my mind was flooded with good memories of how it was before her mental problems kicked in.

The bus driver pulled to a stop on Brocket Road and I
got off.

I hustled over to our place, and as I stepped inside the
door, I stood in shock. Our apartment was in complete
disarray. The television was on the floor, the coffee table
was upside down, and Nana's prized bookshelf was leaning against the back of the sofa with all of the books
strewn every which way. Our home looked like a mini hurricane had come through it and tried to blow it down.

I walked in and stepped over the chaos and made a
beeline for my bedroom. I snatched up the pants I wore
yesterday from the hamper and rummaged through my
pockets. The envelope the general had given me wasn't
there. Then I remembered I had pulled it out and stuffed
it in my sweat-suit pocket on my way to practice. I located
the sweats and felt the paper in the pocket. There it was. I
hated to leave our place like this, but I had bigger fish to
fry. I stepped over the drama that was now our living room
and headed back out the door.

I ran down the steps, and just as I placed my feet on the
sidewalk, I saw Kwame making his way toward our apartment. With the quickness of a cat, I ducked back between
the buildings and turned around to walk through the back
way. I looked around to make sure the coast was clear and
hurried over to Amir's building.

Amir was outside arguing with someone about not signing his petition.

"Not only am I not signing that raggedy paper, I'ma kick
your lil black butt if they close the liquor stores round
here on account of you," the resident said.

"Well fine, then. Be a drunk all your life," Amir spat back.

"I plan on it," the man said, raising his hand in a mock toast.

"What about you?" Amir said, turning to someone else as they walked by. "Help me close these liquor stores down round here. Just sign the petition."

"Them liquor stores ain't bothering nobody," the person said, and kept walking.

"Oh, yes, they are. Look at your teeth," Amir said. "Your liver is going to shrivel up and come out when you cough."

"What's up, man?" I said, walking over to Amir.

"Hey, Rome," he said, shaking his head with a frown. "You alright?"

"Yeah, I'm good. The house is jacked up. Did you see anything?"

"Nah, I went over there looking for you, and that old funky security guard made me leave. Like he was gonna do something. I should've slapped him. What's going on?"

I sighed and blew out a big breath. "I don't know. But I gotta find out. Kwame tryna play superdetective and won't let me help, but I'm not sitting around and waiting on him to try and save the day. He doesn't need to be getting in no trouble anyway. He just got out of trouble."

"Well, what's the plan?" Amir said, turning to a passer-by. "Hey, I need you to sign this petition to close all these liquor stores around here."

"Boy, you crazy? I like the liquor stores around here. Gas too high to be going all over town to get my medicine," the guy said, and kept walking.

"Medicine? What kind of medicine they sell in the liquor store?"

"The kind I need to make me feel like a million bucks," the man said over his shoulder.

"Lazy bastard. Yeah, you need some medicine alright. Some antistupid potion. I hate black people, man. I swear, I wish I was born in Cuba or someplace," he said, frowning at the man who walked off.

He turned back to me.

"Man, you are completely retarded. You know that, don't you?" I said.

"I got two signatures, Romeo. Two. That's why things don't change round here. People too comfortable with their ignorance. And one of the signatures I got from you. My own momma wouldn't even sign the doggone thing. How are we ever going to get out of the hood if so many of us are happy to be here?"

I couldn't deal with Amir's Jesse Jackson act today. I fanned him off and walked away.

"Wait up, Rome," he said, coming after me.

"Man, I gotta find out what's going on with my mom. You go ahead and do your thing," I said.

"Nah, I'm good. These fools round here ain't gonna do nothing," he said, balling up his petition and tossing it in the trash can. "I'm with you. What's the plan?"

"First thing we need to do is find out who this is," I said, unfolding the envelope so we could see the address.

H. W. Warship
245 Harrington Way
Atlanta, GA 30031

"Who is that?" Amir asked.

"That's what we need to find out. General Mack gave it to me. He told me Pearl was in trouble, and she ended up in the hospital all beat up."

"I know you ain't about to go on no wild-goose chase on that fruit loop's word," Amir said. "Tell me you got something with a little more credibility?"

"Nah, I don't but General Mack's been on point lately. He's the one who found her, and he also gave me an envelope with this address that I should have checked out."

"Let's go back to my spot. We can go to MapQuest and find out what's the deal with that address."

"Let's go," I said, anxious to get this thing started.

As we were headed to Amir's house, I saw Kwame. He didn't see me, so I grabbed Amir's arm and we ducked behind the Dumpster.

"What's wrong, bro?" he said, looking at me like I was crazy.

"I told you he wants me to stay out of it. I'm supposed to be at the hospital with Nana and Pearl," I said in a hushed tone.

We watched as Kwame headed through the breezeway. Once he was out of sight, we hustled over to Amir's place. We burst through the door like we were the police and headed straight for his room. Amir logged on to his computer and we pulled up the address. It was in Buckhead, the ritzy downtown area of Atlanta.

"Let's go," I said.

"Man, we need to borrow somebody's car. We can't be doing surveillance on the MARTA bus," Amir said, snatching the directions off the printer.

I thought for a second. He was right. Where could we find a car? I placed my finger on my temple and thought for a few seconds.

"Let's see if we can borrow Mr. Harold's car," I suggested.

"Man, Mr. Harold has been out there all day shooting that gun. He's on the war path. I'm surprised the police haven't come over and locked him up. No, I'm not. Take that right back. Sorry DeKalb County cops ain't good for nothing. But now might not be a good time to be tryna borrow no car from him," Amir said.

"Come on," I said, ignoring Amir.

My cell phone rang and I looked at my home number on the screen.

"Hello," I said.

"Are you by Nana?" Kwame asked.

"Ahh . . . nah. She's still talking to the people," I lied.

"Somebody ransacked the house," he said.

"Whatchu mean?" I said, trying to act like I didn't know what was going on.

"Did Nana say anything about the house?"

"Nah."

"Okay. Try to keep her up there for as long as you can. I don't want her coming home to this mess."

"Okay," I said.

"Where did you put that address?"

"In my jeans. The Sean Johns," I said, keeping the lie going.

"A'ight. I'll holla at you later," Kwame said. "Oh, Romeo."

"Yeah," I said.

"I'm sorry about putting my hands on you. It's just that

I don't want you getting into any trouble. You're on the right track and I wanna keep you on it."

"A'ight," I said, closing the phone without a good-bye.

I stood there for a minute, not sure what to do. Kwame was right; I had no idea what I was getting myself into. Maybe I needed to head back to the hospital and call it a day.

"What's up, man? You look like you are a little confused. Whatcha gonna do, barbeque or mildew?" Amir said.

"Let's get out of here," I said, making up my mind to right some of the wrongs I had done to my mother.

We had to take the long route to Mr. Harold's to avoid bumping into Kwame.

Mr. Harold was sitting in a rocking chair on his front porch. He was in his usual old-man attire—a pair of khaki shorts, a wife-beater T-shirt, and a pair of dress shoes with white dress socks. He was sleeping peacefully with his double-barrel shotgun resting on his lap. His finger wasn't on the trigger, which gave me a little more confidence to approach the sleeping lion. I looked down at his feet and noticed a half-finished bottle of Jack Daniels, and that caused me to pause. There was nothing worse than dealing with an armed drunk.

I approached him with caution. I didn't want him to wake up in a drunken haze and mistake me for some thief and pop off one of those barrels.

"Mr. Harold," I said, in almost a whisper.

Mr. Harold opened one of his eyes, then opened the other one. He furrowed his brows, and then I could see that his drunken brain recognized my face.

"Hey, baby boy," he said, jumping to his feet. "What you doing sneaking up on me?"

"I'm not sneaking up on you. I just came by to check on you. How you doing?"

"I'll be better when I find out who robbed me. I'm okay. Hey there, Amir," Mr. Harold said, staggering back to keep his balance.

"Hey, Mr. Harold. I'm sorry to hear about your house getting robbed," Amir said.

"Won't happen again, I'll tell you that much," he said, tapping his gun. He fell back down into his rocking chair. "Whatchu youngins want? I might be drunk, but I ain't slow. Y'all up to something."

"We need to borrow—" Amir started, but I stopped him.

"Mr. Harold. Somebody beat my mom up pretty bad. They put her in the hospital and Nana's all upset."

He cocked his gun and put a mean mug on his old leathered face. "Who got Beatrice upset?" he barked.

"I don't know. That's what we're tryna find out. We were wondering if we could borrow your car. See, Nana needs a ride to the hospital. You know how she hates riding on those buses," I said, trying to work his love for my nana.

I wouldn't dare tell the truth because the mere utterance of the general's name would automatically make Mr. Harold turn us down.

"Hold on," Mr. Harold said, turning and staggering into his house. He returned a few minutes later and tossed me the keys to his prized Cadillac DeVille. "Bring it back in one piece. I don't give a doggone how y'all lil butts come back, but Beatrice and my car better not have a scratch on them. Insurance and registration in the glove box," he said as he plopped back down in his rocking chair and closed his eyes.

"Thanks, Mr. Harold," I said. "We'll take good care of your car and Nana."

"Um-huh," he said, and went back to his rocking.

23

ROMEO

Amir and I jumped into Mr. Harold's late-model spiffy-clean Cadillac and buckled up. A light drizzle started just as we backed out of the driveway.

"So have you guys called the police?" Amir asked.

"I haven't. I don't think that Kwame called, but Nana might've. But forget the police. They don't solve anything. All they gonna do is take a report. They don't really care about us. You know that."

"Yeah, I think most of them join the police department just so they can get some free clothes," Amir said.

We jumped on Highway 78, then dipped onto I-285 and took that to Interstate 85, and headed north toward Buckhead.

"As crazy as today has been, I think it might be the best day of my life," I said with a smile.

Amir looked at me with a twisted frown.

"I found out today that Pearl was never on drugs. She has some mental problems but not drugs."

"For real?" Amir said. "Hey, watch out, man!" he screamed as I barely missed hitting a car driving in the lane next to me.

"Whoa," I said, snatching the car back into the middle of my lane.

"Oh, heck no. Pull over," Amir said, already undoing his seat belt. "I forgot you can't drive."

I pulled over and didn't have a problem relinquishing my driving privileges. Driving made me nervous, and Amir had been driving his mother around since he was old enough to see over the steering wheel. Not that he ever grew enough to truly see over the steering wheel, but he was still a better driver than I was.

I jumped out and walked around the back of the car to the passenger side. A police siren went off just as I closed the door. I looked back and saw that a Georgia State trooper had pulled up behind us.

"You got your license?" I asked.

"Yeah," Amir said, looking at me like he couldn't believe he was going to get a ticket for something I did.

"Good, because I don't have one," I said, opening the glove compartment. The first thing I saw was a big black pistol. I snatched it out and dropped it on the floorboard. I pushed the gun under the seat with my foot and tried to remain calm.

"Mr. Harold is off the chain. How many guns does that fool have?" Amir said.

The trooper tapped on the window and Amir let it down.

"Is everything alright with you gentlemen?" he asked in heavy Southern drawl.

"Yes, sir. My neighbor let us borrow his car, and I couldn't figure out how to turn on the windshield wipers. So I pulled over to figure it out. Looks like it's about to start pouring down out here," Amir lied with ease. "But we got it now."

"Let me see your license and registration if you don't mind," he said.

Amir handed the officer the documents, and he walked back to his patrol car.

" 'If you don't mind,' " Amir said with a twisted lip. "As if I had a choice. You know I don't like cops, Romeo?"

"I know. Black people, Mexicans, and cops. I got it, bro," I said.

A few minutes later, the officer came back and tapped on the window. He handed Amir his paperwork. "You boys have a good evening," he said. "And be careful out here."

"Thanks and you do the same," Amir said, rolling the window back up.

"See, if that was a black cop, we would've been locked up. It's a shame you can't trust your own people."

"Man, shut up. If a black cop did the same thing that guy did, you would've said, 'If that was a white cop, we would've been locked up.' "

"You're right. All of 'em suck. I hate cops."

I shook my head. Amir pulled back onto I-85. We exited at Cheshire Bridge Road and turned onto Lenox Road. We followed the directions, staying on Lenox until we came to a stop in front of some expensive-looking condominiums.

THE VANDERBILT said the big black letters on the stucco wall, which was surrounded by lots of flowers and shrubbery.

A large iron fence with gold tips surrounded the place.

"Now *that's* a gated community," Amir said. "That crap

they are building around our place looks like a mini prison. I'm thinking about tearing it down myself."

I noticed a car in the entryway, stopped in front of a gate. An arm was hanging out of the driver's side, punching some numbers into a little silver box.

"Pull over," I said. "I'ma get out right here. Park over there in that lot, and if I'm not back in fifteen minutes, call Kwame."

"You sure, Rome?"

"Yeah," I said. "I just wanna get a look around."

"Man, look around at what?"

"I don't know, Amir. I just wanna see what I can see."

"And you talking about Kwame out here tryna play detective. What are you gonna do with what you see?"

"I'm not sure," I said, then reached under the seat and grabbed Mr. Harold's gun.

"Now, why you think you need that?" Amir said.

"If you saw what they did to Pearl, you would take it too," I said.

"I say if you're just going to look around, then you don't need a gun," Amir said. "Guns ain't nothing but trouble, Romeo. I'm serious right now."

"You might be right, but forget that. I'd rather be caught with it than without it."

"A'ight, man. Just remember we're going places, brah. Me and you," Amir said with a serious expression. "Don't do anything dumb."

I held his gaze and balled up a fist. We tapped knuckles and shared a brotherly moment. I think we both knew that we were walking on shaky ground.

"I got you. Just checking the place out. I'll see you in a minute," I said as I exited the car.

I placed the gun in the small of my back and scanned the grounds. I felt strange and out of place. I knew I was just being paranoid, but I could've sworn the entire city of Buckhead was looking at me. And I definitely regretted bringing the gun. It was quite uncomfortable, poking me in the back. I had never even held a gun in my hands, and now I was walking around with one as if I was a gangster. I had a feeling this wasn't going to turn out good.

Amir drove around the little curved driveway and rolled the window down.

"Be smart, Rome," he said before pulling out into traffic.

I headed down the sidewalk in front of the homes, passing an old white lady who was out walking a dog in the drizzle. I did a double take. The dog looked just like the lady and that wasn't a good thing.

"Good evening," I said.

"Good evening to you, young man," she replied pleasantly.

"Good-looking dog," I lied.

I don't know why I felt the need to be extra nice to older people, but I did.

"Thank you," she said. "We've been together for almost fifteen years," she said proudly.

I stopped. Took a knee and rubbed the little ugly dog's head. "That's a long time. You must treat him well."

"Oh, yes. Nothing is too good for my Webster. He keeps me company now that all of my grandkids are out living their lives."

I stood and noticed she already had a foot on the path to where the walkers entered the premises.

"Well, take care and keep up the good work with Webster," I said, walking in front of her down the path. When I got to the pad, I punched in some bogus code.

The old lady walked up. "Are you having a problem?"

"Yes, ma'am. I must've forgotten the code, and my aunt isn't home. I'm here visiting from Florida. I'm thinking about going to Georgia Tech to play football. Do you know where I can find a phone around here so I can call her and get the right code?"

"No need for that. I'll let you in. I hope you have the key to get into the house. It's about to storm pretty hard out here," she said.

"Yes, ma'am." I pulled out my key from the Village and waved it in front of her.

She punched in the code and I heard the locks click open. The small walk-through gate swung open. I allowed her and Webster to enter; then I walked in behind her.

"Thank you. You're a very nice young man, and Georgia Tech is a great school. Both of my sons graduated from Tech, and I have a granddaughter who'll be attending in the fall. Hopefully I'll get a chance to see her from time to time, but probably not. Can't say I blame her too much. What I would do to be eighteen again. "

"Well, I'm sure she'll visit you often." I nodded at her. "Okay, well, thanks again. I better get in the house before it starts raining too hard."

"Yes, it looks like the storm is fast approaching."

"I'm sorry. My name is Jeremy." I reached out to shake her hand. "Here you are helping me out and I'm being rude."

"No no no. You're fine," she said, taking my hand in her brittle pale hands. "Martha Wells, and I'm thankful for the company."

"Well, it was nice meeting you, Mrs. Wells."

"It was nice meeting you, too, young man. Go, Yellow Jackets." She pumped her fist, looking like she was about to throw her arm out of its socket.

I smiled. "Take care. Bye, Webster," I said, waving at the dog.

I walked the opposite way from where Mrs. Wells was headed. I looked at the signs, searching for Harrington Way. I walked over two more streets and there it was. I searched the numbers at the top of each entrance until I saw 245 in big gold letters. Directly in front of the door was the white Hummer.

Now what? I wondered.

What was I going to do now, knock on the door and say, "Why you beat up Pearl, man? And why did y'all fools tear up my nana's house?"

A door beneath the big gold letters opened, and a white guy who looked like he ate people for a living came out. He was followed by an even bigger black man. They were laughing about something. I turned and walked away with my heart racing.

The rain started falling and I heard the truck's alarm beep. They opened the doors to the Hummer, and both of them got in. I counted the doors and walked toward the back of the building. I turned to make sure the Hummer had pulled off before I headed around to the back. Once the car was out of sight, I counted the back doors, then stopped at the third one.

A large French patio door allowed me to see everything inside. The dining room area was packed with red and white cardboard signs. The place looked like it was the headquarters for somebody's campaign. I saw a tall black man walking and talking on the telephone. I jumped back to make sure he didn't see me before peering in for a closer look. He looked familiar, but I couldn't put a finger on where I had seen him.

"Hey," said the large white guy who had just gotten into the Hummer. He slapped a big paw down on my shoulder. "What are you doing?"

Panic kicked in and I realized I had had enough peeking for one day. I took off running. The white guy gave chase, but he was no match for me as I easily sprinted away from him.

I made it toward the main street and saw the Hummer flying toward me. I'm fast but not that fast. The Hummer screeched to a halt and the white guy jumped in.

I leaped over the gate, which gave me a little breathing room, but that didn't last long because as soon as I looked back, I saw the Hummer headed toward me again.

I looked around for Amir as I ran, but he wasn't where I had asked him to be. I was trapped on a long street with nothing but tall fences on both sides. If I didn't think of something quick, I was gonna get caught, and if these were the same people who assaulted Pearl, then I knew I was in trouble. I was scared out of my mind, and all I could think of was, why didn't I let Kwame handle this mess?

The Hummer was fast approaching. I crossed the street and saw Amir. He was half hanging out the window talking to some preppy-looking Asian girl who was doing a fine job of ignoring him.

"Amir!" I screamed.

He didn't even look up.

The Hummer was weaving in and out of cars, heading toward me.

"Amir!" I screamed again, still running toward him. I saw him look at me; then his head popped back in the car. Mr. Harold's car picked up speed as it raced toward me. Just as I made it to the car, the Hummer came out of nowhere and crashed into the front of Mr. Harold's prized Cadillac.

Oh, damn, I thought.

The black guy jumped out and came at me. "Hey, come here," he yelled.

I jumped into the car and he jumped back into the Hummer.

"Back up. Let's get out of here, man," I said.

"What did you do, Rome? Man, I'ma 'bout to die," Amir cried as he tried to put the car in reverse.

I felt a violent crash and my head snapped back.

The Hummer rammed into us and pushed us into the traffic. Tires screeched as a car coming through the intersection tried to avoid hitting us but to no avail.

Boom. Right into the passenger side door.

I could see the whites of the driver's eyes and he screamed in pain.

"These boys ain't playing. Let's bail outta here," I said.

"What the hell you done got me into?" Amir cried again. "I should've stayed home. Ahhhhhhhhh," he moaned in fear. "I hate you, Romeo. I hate you, man."

"Stop crying and get outta the car." I pushed Amir.

He was really boo-hooing now.

"Get out." I kicked him with my foot.

Amir finally got a move on, and we abandoned Mr.

Harold's car, taking off on foot. A gunshot echoed behind us, and that put a whole lot of pep in our step.

"Ahhhhhh," Amir cried. "I don't wanna die. Ahhhhhh. I don't wanna die."

I had to come up with something to get us outta there.

"Come on, Amir," I said, looking back at him struggling to keep up. He was way faster than me, but he was a mess, so his brain wasn't telling his feet to move quickly enough.

We were in the middle of a busy intersection, and the Hummer was blowing its horn and still trying to get to us.

I saw a young black guy sitting behind the wheel of a brand-new Chevrolet Camaro, bobbing his head to some hip-hop track and rubbernecking at all the chaos about him. He looked like he'd seen a ghost when I knocked on his window.

"What's up?" he said.

"Man, we are in trouble. Those guys tried to kill my mother and now they are trying to get me," I said.

"Yo," he said, his eyes lighting up. "Are you Romeo the football player?"

"Yes, but if I don't get outta here, I'ma be a dead man."

"I see," he said, eyeing the guys coming at us. "Get in."

I ran around and opened the passenger door. I held the seat up for Amir to get in the back. Then the guy sped off as if he were on a NASCAR track.

"You played my brother the other night," he said nonchalantly, as if this was an everyday thing for him. "He said you were cool peeps."

"Who is your brother?" I asked, looking back to see where the Hummer boys were.

"Ricky Baxter. I'm Trent."

"Oh, yeah, Rick's cool," I said, trying to catch my breath.

"I can't believe these fools shot at us, man. What in the world kind of foolishness is my mom caught up in?" I said more to myself than to anyone else.

"Where y'all headed?" Trent asked.

"Hey, Romeo," Amir screamed at me. "I'm scared, man."

"Hey, boy," Trent snapped, looking in his rearview mirror. "Stop all that damn screaming in my car."

Amir frowned and started crying.

The Hummer weaved through more traffic and came after us.

Trent smiled and gunned the engine. I couldn't even think straight. Here I was in a life-or-death situation because I hadn't listened to my brother. Trent seemed to be enjoying testing his engine in a real-life situation. He pressed the gas a little too hard and almost ran into a car in front of him that was turning. He slammed on the brakes. Once the car was out of the way, he floored it and ran through every red light he saw. He drove like a madman, but I was grateful because those Hummer boys weren't letting up. They were on our tail every step of the way.

"Man, they ain't going away, Rome," Amir screamed. "We gonna die. I don't wanna die. Geezus, I swear that I will stop watching all that porn, and I promise you I will come to church every Sunday. I'ma join the choir. I swear I will."

Trent chuckled and shook his head. "Where are you guys headed?" he asked again, still as calm as a seasoned getaway driver.

"Tucker, if you can get us there."

"Where in Tucker?"

"Over by Strokers," I said. Every black person in Atlanta knew about the famous gentlemen's club.

"Gotcha," Trent said. "Who are those guys?"

"I don't know. They beat up my mom and I came to see who they were, but they don't seem to be in a talking mood."

"I see," Trent said as he gunned the engine of the powerful sports car. "I'll get you guys home."

In no time at all, I had gone from a promising scholar athlete to a scared little boy who wanted his nana.

24

KWAME

"Talk to me," the man answered the phone.

"May I speak to Priest Dupree?" I said, hoping I had the right number.

"This is he. Who am I speaking to?"

"I don't know if you remember me, but my name is Kwame Braxton. I used to—"

"Yeah, you played football over at Tucker. Quarterback. Got in a bunch of trouble behind some dumbness."

"Yes, that would be me."

"Well, I see that you are calling me from a local number, which means you're out of the pen. Unless you got your hands on a cell phone."

"No, I'm home," I said, already hating having to defend myself. "But I have some problems that I really need your help with."

"I'm listening."

Priest Dupree was a mentor to all the inner-city kids. He

was also a highly decorated police officer who was known to bring down the baddest of the bad. He had a heart of gold but could get gritty when the time called for it. He was the only person I thought of when I decided to go after my mother's tormentors.

"Someone beat up my mother, but we don't think it's your typical street fight."

"What makes you say that?"

"Well, a guy from the neighborhood said he saw two well-dressed guys dump her out of a truck—after they beat her half to death. They were driving a Hummer. The guy got the license plate number. So I was calling to see if you could help me out."

Priest sighed as if he was saying, "Here I go again."

"What's your mother's name?"

"Pearl Braxton."

"That's right. I know Pearl. Haven't seen her in ages. Okay, what's the plate number?"

"Georgia plates NXT 111."

"Give me a few minutes and I'll call you back," Priest said.

"Oh, Priest. The apartment is trashed too."

"What do you mean it's trashed?"

"It's trashed. Everything is tossed."

"You have any idea what they were looking for?"

"Nah, man."

"Have you called the police?"

"No, should I call them?"

"Ah, yeah," Priest said as if I wasn't the brightest bulb in the chandelier.

But the truth was, I hated the police. They were never

friends of mine or anyone like me. I could see them now, trying to twist things around as they tried to put me into this mess merely because I just came home from prison.

"Okay, I'll call them."

"A'ight. Let me see what I can dig up. I'll hit you back on this number you called me from."

I hung up the telephone and picked it back up. I dialed Romeo's cell number.

I got the voice mail. I hung up and lifted the bookshelf from the back of the sofa. I started putting the books back in place when the phone rang.

"Hello," I said.

"Hey, baby," Nana said. "You doing okay?"

"Yes, ma'am. How's everything up there?"

"Your momma's still sleeping. They got her so drugged up she can't talk straight. Lords knows I hate seeing her like this, but God knows what's best."

"Yeah," I said.

"Is Romeo there?"

"No, I left him up there with you," I said.

"He left a long time ago," Nana said, exasperated, as if she could not deal with any more drama. "You haven't seen him at all?"

"No, ma'am, but I'm sure he's on the way."

"Tell him I said, to make sure he calls his job if he's not going to make it in," Nana said.

"I will," I said, seething inside. I knew I saw that boy trying to duck behind the building. I let it go because I figured he wouldn't lie to me about being at the hospital. "Okay, Nana, let me straighten up around here."

"Okay, I'ma stay with Pearl for a spell."

"I'll be up there a little later on."

"Kwame, make sure you tell Romeo what I said."

"Yes, ma'am. I'll talk to you later."

I hung up the phone, and before I could pick up the receiver, it rang.

"Kwame, we in trouble, man," was the first thing I heard.

"Who is this?"

"This Amir. We're running from somebody."

"What do you mean you're running—?"

"Come on, man, I can't get into that right now. Hey, man, watch out," Amir yelled. "Man, we on the way to the crib. Get us some help, man. We got somebody on our butts."

I heard Romeo in the background saying something, and I could tell they were in a panic.

"Romeo said it's the guys in the Hummer," Amir said.

I could hear the fear oozing from Amir's breath.

"Y'all get here right now. I'll be outside waiting."

"We're in a blue Camaro, man," Amir said before hanging up.

After hanging up, I made a beeline for the front door. My heart was pumping overtime, and all I could think of was protecting my little brother. Just as I made it to the front door, I heard the phone ring. I turned around and snatched the receiver up to my ear.

"Yeah," I said.

"Kwame, this is Priest. Got a little info. The Hummer belongs to a man named Harry Warship. Does that name right a bell?"

"No."

Priest was quiet for a moment, as if trying to figure out how to continue.

"Hmm, okay. Well, he's some big-shot real estate guy. Now he's trying to dip into politics."

"Okay," I said, still not following why this man would want to hurt my mother. "Priest, I hate to rush you off, but I just found out right now that my brother is running from the same guys who drove that Hummer. I don't know what he done got himself into, but it doesn't sound good. They're headed here right now. You think you can get over here?"

"I'm less than an hour away," Priest said. "Ask your nana about Mr. Warship. And call the police."

"Thanks," I said, hanging up the phone. I skipped the call to the authorities and rushed from our wrecked home.

I ran through the breezeway and bumped into Mr. Harold.

"Hey, boy," the old man said. "How you doing?"

"I'm good, Mr. Harold. In a little rush right now."

"Have you seen my car? Somebody broke into my house, but I could've sworn my car was there. I think I was driving it, but I'm not sure. I do remember two guys coming up to me, but I'm not sure if they stole the car or not. Man, this old age is a mess."

Yeah, but I'm sure that liquor doesn't help, I thought.

"I guess I'll just call the police and report it stolen too. Doggone hoodlums will steal the stink off of dog dung."

"I understand. Well, good luck with that, Mr. Harold," I said as I ran off from the old man. I headed across the grass toward the playground and stood by the street, hoping to see Romeo.

As I waited, I looked back over at the playground and saw Wicked. He was talking to some girl while his flunkies lingered around in the background waiting on him to give a command.

I turned and jogged over to him.

"Let me holla at you," I said.

He looked at me, then turned away and kept talking to the girl.

"Yo, man, I need to talk to you," I barked. "I need your help. Romeo got some drama," I said, turning my head when I heard a car skidding around the corner toward us. "Come on, man," I said to Wicked.

He didn't ask a question, just jumped his big butt up and followed me to the corner.

I saw a navy blue Camaro come flying into the complex, and I noticed Romeo in the passenger seat. The car came to a stop, and Romeo and Amir jumped from it. They didn't see me nor hear me as I yelled Romeo's name. They hit the ground running like the Devil himself was on their tails. The Camaro slammed into reverse and shifted into drive and barely missed a white Hummer as it came barreling into the driveway. Two big guys jumped out and gave chase to Romeo and Amir. Then my life turned upside down and my world stopped. I witnessed my little brother turn around and fire a gun at the men who were chasing him.

Boom!

The black guy screamed and fell to the ground, holding his leg.

"Oh, my God" was all I could say. I knew I hadn't seen what I thought I just saw. Did my little brother just shoot someone? I was paralyzed with fear of losing him to the same hell from which I had just come.

Wicked pulled out his own gun and let one off in the air.

Romeo and Amir kept running.

The white guy stopped in his tracks and gave a menacing glare in our direction. He kept his eyes on us as he walked over to where the black guy was holding his leg.

Wicked let off another shot for good measure.

"What the problem is?" Wicked said with his pistol vacillating between the two men.

"Whoa," the white guy said, slowly removing a badge from his belt. "We're police officers."

"What I care about that Mickey Mouse badge, potna?" Wicked said, never lowering his gun. "If you were legit, this place would be swarming with blue lights right about now. So I ain't about to fall for that Captain Crunch brass. Now, I ask again. What the problem is?"

The white guy held up his hand. "Everybody, calm down. This is official police business."

"What kind of official police business you got beating up women? Chasing little boys?" I said.

The two Hummer guys looked at each other. The black guy limped to his feet. They tried to back away toward their vehicle.

"You tell those little bastards I said the next time we catch them snooping around places they don't have any business, it's not going to turn out good for them," the black guy said.

"Why don't you tell them?" Wicked said with his huge Desert Eagle gun still trained on them.

"Young man, put that gun away," the white guy said. "You have no idea who you're dealing with."

"Ask me if I really care." Then Wicked called out to his

cronies, "Get in that truck and take it to the spot." Wicked was careful not to use any of his boys' names.

"Are you crazy? Young man, you make a move toward that vehicle and I'll shoot you," the white Hummer guy said.

"Man, you're an arrogant lil something, ain't cha? Here I am pointing a big ol' gun at you, and you still think you can get to yours before I pull this trigger. Boy, I will splatter pork all over these here streets if you test me. Now, if you say another word, I'ma shoot *you*," Wicked said.

"That's it. This is not a game," the white guy screamed. "Hey, stay away from that vehicle," he said, turning to the Hummer. "If you get in that car, you will be committing a felony."

His plea landed on deaf ears. One of Wicked's boys jumped in the Hummer and drove off as if the vehicle belonged to him.

The black guy reached for his gun, and one of Wicked's guys aimed a pistol at him. "I wouldn't do that if I was you, homie," he said with a smile.

"I got these fools," Wicked said. "Now drop y'all little guns on the ground."

"Does this look like a movie to you?" the black guy said. "I'm a detective with the Atlanta Police Department, and I refuse to play this game with you, son."

"I don't act in movies and I'm not your son. Now, if you say one more word, I'm gonna show you I mean business. What you wanna do with 'em, homie?" Wicked said, turning to me.

"Get 'em in a house somewhere and I'll holla at you in a minute," I said, ready to get to my little brother, all the while hoping Wicked wouldn't do nothing stupid.

25

KWAME

I walked in the door and saw my little brother sitting on the sofa. His head was in his hands, and he was nervously rocking back and forth. Tears were streaming down his dark cheeks, and I couldn't bring myself to be mad at him. He looked like the same scared little boy I had to protect when some older kids threatened to take his shoes when he ventured off into one of our rival neighborhoods. I wasn't having it then and I wasn't going to have it now.

Romeo looked at me and jumped up, going into a defensive posture. I could tell he was preparing himself to get smacked into next year, but I was never the type to kick a man while he was down. I walked over to him and placed a hand on his shoulder. He jumped back and I had never felt so bad in my life.

"You okay?" I asked.

He nodded, but I could smell the fear emanating from his skin.

"Where's your partner in crime?" I asked.

"He went home."

"Okay. Talk to me. Tell me everything that happened."

He gave me the entire rundown, from the time he ducked behind the building trying to avoid me to the time when he came screeching back to the hood.

"That wasn't smart, Romeo. But what's done is done. Do you know somebody named Harry Warship?"

"Nah." He hesitated.

He looked like he was searching his brain. He frowned as his brain scanned his memory bank; then his eyes lit up. "I know that name. That's the name that was on those posters in the house I was at. Yeah, I saw him. I was at his house. The guys who were chasing us were at his house too."

"Let's talk while we clean up," I said, trying my best to keep my cool. My mind was racing a million miles per hour as I thought of my next move. What was I going to tell Wicked to do with the guys? What would I tell my grandmother? How would I get to the bottom of this whole saga while keeping my little brother out of jail?

I snuck a peek at Romeo and saw he was barely hanging on. He kept wiping his eyes, but as soon as he cleared away the wetness, a new set of tears moisturized his cheeks. I knew I had to be strong for both of us. We started putting things back into the drawers, replacing books and trying to get the house back in order.

"Come on, man. Get a move on," I said when I saw him looking at me crazy. I was trying to keep him moving to keep his thoughts off of his dumb moves.

"What happened to the men who were chasing us?" he asked.

"You *should* be worried about yourself. Mr. Harold is

out there looking for his car. Said two guys came up and took it while he was asleep. He was a little too drunk to remember, but I would've never thought it was you and Amir."

He dropped his head. "We didn't take his car—he gave us the keys."

"So where's the man's car?"

"Those fools in the Hummer crashed it all up," he said, then started crying again. "I don't know why they started tripping so hard, but they tried to kill us. They rammed into Mr. Harold's car and pushed us out into the middle of the intersection over there by Lenox Road and Buford Highway. Cars were coming from everywhere. It's a wonder I'm still here talking to you."

"You should've stayed at the hospital, Romeo," I said, trying my best not to choke my little brother for his stupidity.

"I know, but, man, I couldn't sit there and do nothing. I mean, now that we know Pearl is not on that stuff, we gotta look after her."

"Mr. Harold is going to report his car stolen, and those men are going to want some answers for you shooting one of them. Why did you do that?"

"I was scared. They were shooting at us."

I felt myself getting angrier at Romeo, but then I got distracted by a jingling of the door handle. The door opened and in walked Nana.

"What in the world happened to my house?" Nana said, looking at the major mess her apartment had become. "Oh, my goodness."

"Nana, who is Harry Warship?" I asked.

"Who?"

"Does that name ring a bell?" I pressed.

"Y'all boys better tell me what happened to my house or I'ma go on a warpath."

"Somebody came in here and tossed the place up. We think the people were working for this Harry Warship guy. Seems to me they were looking for something. Do you know what they could be after?" I asked.

"I don't know what that man was looking for, but he ain't gonna find it in here," she said as she immediately went into cleanup mode.

"So you do know him?" I asked.

She fanned me off. "Only God knows what your momma's caught up in," Nana said, lifting a lamp from the table and sitting it upright.

"Okay," I said. "Romeo, *stay* here with Nana. I'll be back in a few. Don't you move a muscle, man. I'm serious," I said, but I doubted it was needed. He was too scared to even go to the bathroom alone.

"Where you going?" Nana asked.

"I gotta run out and check on a few things right quick. I'll be back shortly."

"So nobody's gonna tell me nothing?" Nana said. "Fine. I'll be in my room whenever y'all feel like clueing me in on y'all little shenanigans. And call the police and tell them Harry Warship beat up Pearl."

"Nana," I said, standing by the door. "Who is Harry Warship?"

She sighed and shook her head. She walked into her bedroom and closed the door.

I gave Romeo one last warning look before I left the apartment. It was time to go see what information Wicked had pulled out of the Hummer boys.

26

KWAME

When I walked into the abandoned apartment, what I saw gave me goose bumps and made my stomach turn. Both of the Hummer boys were tied up to their chairs and stripped down to nothing but their underwear and shoes.

Wicked was pacing back and forth with his big gun in his hand. The black guy had a bruised eye, and the white guy's lip looked like it was about to fall into his lap. The first thing that popped into my mind was a bus ride back to prison.

I had to be smart. I held up a finger to let Wicked know that I would be right back. I backed out of the apartment and into the hallway and dialed Priest's number.

"Hello," he answered on the first ring.

"Priest," I said, taking a deep breath. "Seems like I jumped outta the frying pan and back into the fire. My brother went snooping after the guys who beat up our moms, and . . . well, let's just say things are a little deeper now."

"What's up? Talk to me."

"Some kind of way, my little brother found the address to where the guys who beat up Moms stayed. He went looking for them, and he found more than he bargained for. They weren't too happy to see him and chased him off. But they didn't stop there. He said they wrecked up the car he was driving pretty bad and took a few shots at him. He got a ride with somebody back to the crib, but the men chased them all the way home. Some of the local thugs didn't take too kindly to a few outsiders coming in here shooting and carrying on, so they started firing back."

"So get to the bottom. Where are the men now?"

"They're tied up in an abandoned building," I said. "We're in over our heads, man."

"Do you guys even know who the men are?"

I paused before answering the question. "They said they're cops."

"Cops?" he almost screamed. "My God, you boys sure know how to find some trouble, don't you? You said they're tied up?"

"Yeah."

"Go in their pockets and get their identification. I'll hold on while you go and check them out."

I went back to the abandoned apartment. I looked around until I found a pile of clothes in the corner. I picked up the pants and went through the back pocket and came out with a wallet. I did the same for the other pair.

"Hey, I hope you have more sense than your ignorant

little homeboys here," the black guy said. "What you are doing is called obstruction of justice, kidnapping, assaulting a police officer while—"

"Shut up," Wicked snapped. "Did you think you could just bust up in our spot and take one of ours? No, sir. Don't work like that. I know them boys. They ain't done nothing to nobody. Never had and never will. Now, me," Wicked said. "I'ma gangster for sure, and I don't have a problem with popping one in you. Ya hear me?"

I turned and walked out of the room as Wicked played out his ghetto fantasy live and in living color.

"I got it," I said, getting back to Priest. "One of them is named Marvin Gripson and the other one is—"

"Colin Harris. Am I right?"

"Yeah," I said.

"Okay. Got some good news and some bad news. Bad news is they *are* cops. The good news is both of them are a little on the shady side, so whatever you said they did, they probably did it. They must be working extra jobs for Warship."

"So what do we do?" I asked.

"I don't know, but you guys need to let them go. Tell somebody with a car to take them somewhere and drop them off, and do not lay a finger on them."

"Well, it's a little too late for that," I said.

Priest sighed. "Why did I know you were going to say that? I guess expecting two dirty cops to be left alone in the hood is asking too much. Okay, well, get them out of there as safe as you can."

"Hey, Priest. Nana knows Harry Warship, but she's not talking. How do you think she knows him?"

"I'd rather you get that information from her."

"Can you hold on a minute, Priest?" I said, looking at the caller ID as another call came in.

"Nah, you go ahead and do what I asked you to do. I'll call you back in a hot second."

"Okay," I said, clicking over. "Hello."

"Kwame, this Rome. The hospital just called," he said. Then he paused for what seemed like forever. "They said Momma is missing."

27

KWAME

I arrived back at the apartment to find Romeo with his arm around a crying Nana. I guess he had shared with her what he was doing for the last few hours. Before I could walk over to them, there was a knock at the door. I turned to answer it, and when I opened the door, I saw our mother. She looked like a mummy, what with bandages all over her face. I don't know how she got here, but it had to have involved a heavy dose of God.

I reached out for her and she almost collapsed in my arms.

"Oh, Lord, get her in the bedroom," Nana said, getting up from the sofa and walking over to help me. "Romeo, call the hospital and see—"

"No," Pearl said, struggling to pull herself away from me. "They know I'm there. They gonna get me."

"Who knows you're there?" I asked.

"They're gonna kill me," she said.

We all looked at each other. Was Pearl hallucinating or

was this real? Given today's events, we had to assume we were dealing with the sane Pearl.

"Take her in my room," Nana said with a look of pity and compassion on her face.

No rest for the weary, I thought.

I led our mother to Nana's room and helped her onto the bed.

"Mom, what are you caught up in?" I asked.

"I don't want you involved," she said, moaning. "This is my mess."

"Too late for that. We're already involved," I said.

She looked at me and a painful grimace overtook her face. "Y'all don't need to be messing around with this. I'll fix it. I can fix this. Dirty Harrrrrrrrrryyyyyyyy," she screamed.

"Fix what? Mom, tell me something. Who is Harry Warship, and why is he trying to hurt you?" I pleaded.

All of a sudden, she swung her head to the side and looked at the wall. "Harry, you leave my boys alone. You hear me? I said leave them alone or I swear before God that I will tell everything. You can kill me, but the truth will live on."

I watched in amazement as my mother had a conversation with the wall.

Who in the heck is this Harry guy, and why won't anybody tell me anything about him?

I stood upright and stared down at my mother. She looked up and stared right through me.

"Who is Harry Warship, Mom?"

Her eyes widened with surprise; then she closed them and turned onto her side.

"Who is Harry Warship, Mom?" I asked again.

No answer. No response. She was done talking.

I left the room and went back out to the living room with Nana and Romeo.

"Nana, who is Harry Warship?" I asked.

"Why do you keep asking me about that man?"

"Because Momma just asked him to leave her boys alone. We also found out that he was the one who beat her up, or at least had someone beat her up."

"I don't know nothing 'bout no Harry Warship," Nana said.

I huffed and closed my eyes. I tried to rub away the tension that was building between my ears. This was too deep for us. I had to call Priest again.

"Yo," he answered right away.

"Hey, man. I'm sorry to bother you, but my mom left the hospital and she's here now. She said some people were after her. I'm sure it was Mr. Warship, or she's hallucinating."

"I'm about ten minutes away from you guys. I have some solid information. Did you get those guys out of there yet?"

"Nah, I haven't had a chance to do that."

"That's cool. Call your dogs off of those boys in blue. Tell them to just leave them where they are. I'll take it from there."

"I'm on it," I said.

"See you in a few."

I hung up the phone and turned to my brother. "Romeo, stay here. I gotta make a quick run. Lock the door and don't answer it for nobody."

"Baby, why don't you call the police?" Nana suggested.

"The police are already here," I said. "I'm going to talk to them right now."

28

KWAME

I knocked on the door of the apartment where the Hummer boys were being held. Wicked answered with a big smile on his face. He was still carrying his big gun, like he was in the old wild west.

"What's the word?" he asked.

"I need you and your boys to pack it up," I said. "I appreciate you coming through, but I think I got it from here."

"You sure?" he asked, and seemed to be quite disappointed that his time with the dirty cops had come to an end.

"Yeah," I said. "I'm sure."

"Man, I was just about to have a little more fun with them. They got a lot of nerve coming round here with that nonsense. Must think we ain't got no pride or nothing. I already hate cops, and I'll die a slow death before I let one of 'em come on these grounds and try to hurt one of my people."

"I hear you. But go ahead and get your boys to clear outta there," I said.

"What you want me to do with those busters?" he said, pointing toward the cops.

"Leave 'em there," I said flatly.

"A'ight. You're the quarterback. I'm just a hard-hitting linebacker who gets his rocks off causing extraordinary amounts of pain. Some things never change, huh?" Wicked said, turning to go back into the apartment.

"Yo, Wicked," I called before he got inside.

"What's up," he said, turning around to face me.

"We're even. If you hadn't come through, ain't no telling what them boys might've done or what I would've had to do to keep my little brother safe. He might not even be breathing right now if it weren't for you, so thanks, man."

"Kwame, I hear you but I'm not accepting that. Two years of your life don't even begin to add up to one little beat-down. Especially some cops. Dirty cops at that. Man, they were in there talking about who they made disappear. I guess they tryna scare somebody. The more they talked, the more I put that pain on 'em. So, nah, we ain't even. Just call it the thug in me, but we are good when I say we are."

"Nah, we're good," I said.

"Let me ask you a question," Wicked said.

"I'm all ears."

"Was jail fun for you?" he said, getting serious.

"What do you think?"

"Well, a'ight, then. That's all this was to me," he said. "So we ain't even until I say we're even."

I hunched my shoulders and nodded for him to go

ahead and clear out. I turned and walked out onto the sidewalk and waited for Priest.

"Hey," Kelli said, startling me as she snuck up from behind. "I was looking for you."

"Hey," I said nervously, looking over her shoulder toward the place where Wicked was. "What's up?"

"Is everything okay? I heard about your mother and your house getting broken into," she said with concern.

"News travels quick," I said.

"Well, Franky stopped the guy who broke in."

"Who was it that broke in?" I asked.

"Franky said it was some guy named Mark. He said he broke in because Romeo broke into his house and beat him up."

What in the world? Romeo sure has been acting way out of character. Or was I gone so long that this is his character now?

"Yeah, well . . . ," she said, waiting for an answer.

"I think everything's gonna be okay."

"Yo, Kwame, we outta here. You sure you good?" Wicked asked, still holding his gun in the open for the world to see. He was followed by three other guys.

Kelli turned toward him and her eyes went straight to the gun.

"Yeah, I'm good," I said, giving him the eye to keep it moving and wondering why he didn't put that thing away.

"Kwame, what's going on?"

"Nothing. I'm waiting on a cop friend of mine to come over here."

She gave me a quizzical look and nodded.

"I'll come by your place a little later on. Let me get this taken care of first, okay?" I said.

"Okay," Kelli said, reaching out and rubbing my arm. "But you sure everything is okay?"

"Yeah, my mind is just somewhere else right now. I'm sorry."

"I understand. Make sure you come by later. Maybe I can cook something for your mom and we can take it to the hospital?"

"She's home already. It wasn't that bad," I said.

"Oh. Okay," she said, grabbing my hand with both of hers. Her eyes were pleading with me to be careful. She gave my hand a slight squeeze before releasing it. She gave me once last chance to tell her what was going on before walking back to her place.

Priest pulled up in a silver Ford Harley-Davidson F-150 truck. He jumped out looking like a young Muhammad Ali. Six-feet-two-inches tall and a no-nonsense style about him.

"What's happening, little brother?" Priest said, slapping my hand. He gave me a brotherly hug. "It's good to see you. What have you been doing, lifting every weight you could find?"

"I'm stressing, man," I said, motioning for him to follow me. "Thanks for coming."

"Well, let's see what you got going on."

We walked over to the door where the policemen were being held, and Priest peeped in. He came back out and looked at me with a frown on his face. "Who did that?"

"Couple of the locals. I guess they got a little over-excited," I said, shaking my head to let him know I didn't agree with it.

"This is not good, bro." Priest took a deep breath. "I know those men, and they're not just gonna let this go."

My heart skipped a few beats, and I saw myself headed back down that long road to the penitentiary again. The only difference would be that this time my little brother would be sitting beside me because the state would get a great deal of joy out of charging him as an adult.

Priest sighed, then removed his BlackBerry and punched in a few numbers. "Okay," he said. "Go on home. I'll come find you in a minute."

"Okay."

"What apartment are you in?"

"Five seventy-five," I said, hesitating. "But what's—"

Priest shook his head, halting my question as he responded to whatever came back to him in his phone. "Where is that?"

I pointed toward my building.

"I'll see you in a bit. I'm going to try and clean this up as best I can," he said before turning his back to me. His phone rang; then I heard him say, "Mr. Warship, we need to talk."

29

KWAME

I stood in the corner of our apartment, looking out the window, hoping to get a glimpse of what the future would hold. Our home was as quiet as it had ever been. You could hear a pin drop. Nana sat on the sofa reading from her well-worn Bible. Romeo sat on the love seat with his nervous eyes glued to me. The television was on, but the volume was all the way down. There was a rumbling in the rear of the house near Nana's room. A door opened and out came our mother, walking gingerly but with purpose. I rushed over and led her to the sofa.

"Pearl, why don't you sit your behind still somewhere?" Nana scolded.

"Momma, I'm tired of lying down. I need to go take care of some things."

"And how do you think you gonna do that? You can barely walk," Nana said.

"I gotta fix this mess I got my boys in. I know how to fix it," Pearl said.

"No, I think you've done enough already. Now, before you brought your butt around here, everything was fine. You show up and now all hell done broke loose. I'ma tell you this right now. Either you get yourself some help or don't you come back around here no more," Nana said.

Pearl shook her head as she tried to stand. "I know what I'm doing, and nothing you say is gonna stop me from fixing this."

"Girl," Nana snapped, rising to her feet as well. "You better sit you butt down before I knock you down. I'm tired of your foolishness."

For the first time in my life, I saw a mean streak in Nana.

Pearl must've seen it, too, because she eased back down onto the sofa.

There was a knock on the door. I walked over and answered it. It was Priest, and he didn't look happy.

"Who is Harry Warship?" I asked before he could step a foot into the apartment.

"Mind your manners, boy," Nana chastised as she stood and motioned for Priest to come in. "Please forgive my grandson, Priest. He seems to have lost his manners."

"No problem, ma'am," Priest said as he walked in and stopped in the middle of the living room. He stood there looking at Pearl. His face showed nothing. Then he turned to Nana. "Thanks for inviting me in."

Nana nodded.

Priest reached out and shook Nana's hand. He nodded at Romeo and Pearl. "It's been a long time since I've seen you guys. Sorry that it has to be under these circumstances."

"Well, before you get into all of that, can I get you something to drink or eat?" Nana asked.

"No, ma'am. I don't have a lot of time," he said. "I'll get right to it. This situation has gotten way out of hand on both sides, but I'm going to try and mediate this thing so that both parties can walk away with something rather than nothing. How are you doing, Pearl?" he said, looking at our mother.

Pearl looked away.

"Would you like to tell them or should I?" Priest said, looking at Pearl.

"Tell them what?" she spat back. "Ain't nothing to tell. Dirty Harry is a criminal, and you should be over there locking him up instead of standing over me looking crazy. But money talks and poor folks walk, right, Mr. Policeman?"

Priest nodded but then went on. "Tell them why you contacted Harry Warship and what you were trying to accomplish."

Pearl's eyes cut through Priest. If looks could kill, he would've died a thousand deaths. She closed her eyes and didn't reopen them.

"Okay," Priest said. "Harry Warship is going to be the next mayor of Atlanta. That's pretty much a given. He's put in a tremendous amount of work and spent . . . I don't know how much money to make it happen." He paused for what seemed like an eternity. "And he's not about to let the fact that he's both of you guys' father ruin this opportunity that he's created for himself."

Our father? Did I just hear him right? Our father?

Priest let that heavy news sink in as he stood there

studying our faces. I didn't feel anything, but it looked as if Romeo had been hit with a sledgehammer.

"Mr. Warship is running his campaign based on family values." Priest chuckled and shook his head at the absurdity of the notion. "He was—and still is—a married man. Needless to say, if news got out that he had two children out of wedlock, his chances of winning the election would be slim to none. That's where your mother comes in. She contacted him and threatened to go to the press if he didn't give her a million dollars. He balked at it, and from there we are here," Priest said.

"Do you think it's fair that we live like this and he's living like a king?" Pearl snapped. "He owes me every dime I asked for. My kids are no less worthy than the ones he has with that stringy-haired, four-eyed fool he calls a wife."

"Pearl," Nana growled, shutting our mother up.

Priest threw up his hands. "Hey, you get no argument from me. I'm only here to deliver the news and to try and solve this thing before anyone else gets hurt."

"So now what?" Nana said, looking at Pearl like she could kill her.

"Well," Priest said, looking at Romeo, "one of Mr. Warship's men got shot. Seems like he was chasing a trespasser, and the trespasser took offense to being chased and shot him. They, Mr. Warship, want the shooter. Mr. Warship doesn't want this news to get to the media, so he's willing to give you the money you asked for in exchange for the person who shot one of his bodyguards."

"Tell him I want cash," Pearl said. "I wouldn't take a check from Dirty Harry because he dirty."

"What if we don't know who shot his guy?" I said.

"Kwame, I know what you are trying to do, but it's not going to work. The police officer who was shot knows exactly who shot him," Priest said.

"Well, I don't know who shot his little flunky. So that doesn't matter to me. I want my money," Pearl blurted. "It's time for Dirty Harry to pay the piper. He's been getting over too long. Now, tell him I want my money or I'm calling Channel two."

"Romeo, do you know who shot him?" Priest asked.

Romeo looked at Nana and started crying.

"Noooooooooooo!" Nana screamed. "I just got my baby home from jail and I'm not letting another one go. You tell that man to keep his money. We don't need it."

"I wish it was that easy," Priest said. "Cops just don't let people shoot them and get away with it. Someone needs to pay. Now, my advice to you is take the money and use some of it for a good lawyer and move on with your lives. A good lawyer can get these charges dropped to self-defense or maybe even dropped altogether."

"I won't hear of it," Nana said, rushing off to her room with tears in her eyes.

"How much time is he looking at doing?" Pearl said, seemingly oblivious to anything other than counting that money.

"It doesn't matter because he's not going to jail," I said.

Priest looked at me with pity in his eyes. "I'm sorry, Kwame, but I gotta take him."

"You know I can't let you do that, Priest. Now, I didn't call for you to come here and arrest my brother. I called you because I thought you could help us."

"And that's what I'm trying to do," Priest said, making a motion with his eyes at Romeo.

Romeo was quick to take the hint, because he looked around nervously and then jumped up and bolted for the door.

Priest didn't even bother to move, but I had no idea what was going on, so I bum-rushed him into the wall. He was taller than me and just as strong, if not stronger, but he didn't put up the slightest bit of resistance.

Once Romeo was out of the apartment, I backed away from Priest.

"Take me, man," I said. "I'll confess. I'll say I did it."

"Man, you done scuffed up my new shoes," Priest said nonchalantly as he walked past me to the door. "Try to find a good lawyer, Kwame. I may be able to fix this thing so he never sees the inside of a cell, but you'll have to bring him down and get him booked. It's just protocol."

"When am I getting my money?" Pearl said.

"Shut your mouth, girl," Nana said from the rear of the apartment. "And get out of my house."

I looked at Pearl, who was staring at me as if I were a stranger. She closed her eyes, then lay down on the sofa.

God bless her, I thought.

I gave her one last look, then followed Priest out of our apartment.

I was not about to hand my little brother over to the police; I would rather die than have him spend one night in the place I had just given two years of my life to. No, we would have to work out something else. Giving them Romeo was out of the question.

30

ROMEO

I busted out of the apartment, scared out of my wits. I don't know what made me think I could run away from this, but after seeing Priest give me the eye to hit the door, I didn't wait around to ask him any questions.

Why did I turn around and shoot that man? I wondered, the thought continually racking my brain. That one dumb move was going to cost me my life. I was going to the one place I swore to stay away from.

As I ran toward the back of the apartment complex, I looked up at the sky and wondered why God had cursed our family like He did. Why did some people go on with their lives and live happily ever after and my family was always faced with a crisis?

Most of my childhood had been spent worrying about a mother who was out in the streets dealing with demons that made her march up and down the street screaming at billboards. Then, just as Kwame was about to live his dream of playing college football, that was snatched away from him and he was shipped off in chains to prison for something he didn't even do. And now here I was in the worst predicament of my life.

Then I thought about Pearl and how willing she was to give me up for some money. I frowned at the thought. What kind of mother would do such a thing? A schizophrenic one, I guess.

I raced through the breezeway. Behind the very last building in our section of the apartments was where I decided to hide. I leaned against the building to catch my breath and try to plot my next move. I heard a dog barking. The barking was coming closer; then all of a sudden, a pair of paws pressed into my chest and I was up against the building. I closed my eyes and tried to protect myself. When I opened my eyes, I saw a snarling pit ball snapping his teeth at my face.

"Did I decorate your house good enough, playboy?" Mark said as he walked over to me. He seemed to be enjoying my discomfort. He had the dog's leash wrapped around his skinny arm, and he was drinking a bottle of Powerade.

"Hey, man," I said. "Get this dog off of me."

Mark smiled, took a long gulp of his drink, then smiled again.

"Why?"

"Come on, Mark, man," I said as the dog was still daring me to move with his sharp teeth.

"Come on nothing. Who you think you dealing with? You don't bust up into my house acting like you have rights to the place. Then when I ask you a simple question, you haul off and punch me. Nah, bro. It doesn't work like that."

"Hey, man, I'm sorry about that, but somebody beat up my mother and I just wanted to call nine-one-one."

"Oh, now you wanna be sorry. I should give Felony the word and let him make a Happy Meal out of you."

I looked down at the vicious-looking pit bull and sighed.

"Yeah, look at you now," Mark said. "You scared now. You was big and bad before, but look at you now."

"Hey, man, I said I was sorry. I just wanted to get my mom an ambulance."

"Whatchu doing back here?" he asked.

It was hard for me to think with the dog all up in my grill.

"Speak," Mark said.

"I don't know, Mark. I just came back here to think, man. Some people beat up my mom, man."

"Well, I'ma let this lil thing go since I already tore up your lil raggedy house. But don't you ever try to play me no more, boy. I can be a nightmare to you."

"A'ight, man. I apologize."

"Yeah," he said, then he walked away, but the dog was still on me. "Genug," he said. The dog jumped down and ran after Mark. "That's German, boy," he said with a laugh as he walked on about his business.

I breathed a sigh of relief and moved on. I pushed through the overgrown shrubs in the back of the building and found the spot I was looking for.

The building had stairs bolted to the bricks. We used to climb them all the time when we were little. Night had fallen and I couldn't see much of anything back there, but I knew these buildings like the back of my hand. I felt around for the loose step ladder and made sure I skipped it and continued my climb to the top of the building. I could hear police sirens off in the distance, but they were getting closer and I knew they were coming for me.

My heart was sinking further and further out of my chest. I felt around in the small of my back for Mr. Harold's gun. I didn't know what I was gonna do with it, but I felt better having it.

Once I made it to the top of the building, I stayed low so that no one could see me. I eased over to the edge and peered below. What I saw almost gave me a panic attack. The DeKalb Police Department was out in full force. I saw a uniformed police officer talking to Mark and his well-trained dog.

I saw Mark point in the opposite direction of where he just saw me, then he kept walking. I looked to my left and noticed two police officers standing in front of Amir's door. That made me nervous.

Amir was my boy, but he was a scared little something, and I knew it wouldn't take much for the police officers to make him sing like a bird. Before I could even get the thought out of my head, I saw Amir being led from his house in handcuffs. I could hear his mother and his little sister crying inside the apartment.

God, this was almost too much for me to take.

Hearing the horror in the voices of Amir's mother and little sister made me want to come down and turn myself in, but I couldn't do it. Not now. I had to think. I certainly wasn't going to let him take the fall for me, but I had to think. I backed away from the edge and rolled over onto my back. I tried in vain to calm myself. I covered my ears so I could block out the sirens and the cries of my best friend's family, but that wasn't working. I was in purgatory.

I heard my name being called. It was Kwame and he was below me. He had to know I wasn't going to answer him. My cell phone vibrated. I was thankful I had changed the ring tone while I was at the hospital. I quickly snatched it out and looked at the caller ID.

"Ngiai," I whispered.

"She's not pregnant," Ngiai said with excitement rushing from her voice. "I saw her in the mall, and she came up to me and told me. She said her little visitor showed up today. I'm still mad at you and we're still not together anymore, but at least your dumb behind ain't gonna be a daddy."

I placed the phone to my heart. God, what I wouldn't give for a baby to be my only problem. I put the phone to my ear again.

"I'll call you back," I whispered as I pressed the END key before she could say another word.

The phone vibrated again. It was Ngiai. I pressed the END key again, sending it to voice mail. Then I turned the phone off.

The sirens stopped, but the lights were still flashing. I peered over the edge of the building and saw that a few more cars had pulled up.

Why were all of those officers out there? Was what I did that bad? They were coming for me, and they were gonna get me too.

How could I have been so stupid? And why did I go searching for Pearl's tormentors in the first place? Why did I even care? What was I gonna do?

I heard something over by the stairs. I jerked my head in that direction and reached for Mr. Harold's gun, but quickly decided that I wasn't going to use it. I pulled it out and pushed it aside. Closing my eyes, I waited for them to come get me. But then everything went silent again. Then I heard someone yell and a loud thump, followed by more yelling. I eased over to the side of the building and saw two police officers helping one guy back to his feet.

"I don't think he's up there. That ladder is too weak to handle my skinny butt," said the officer who was being helped up.

"I think you're right," one of the other cops said as they moved on.

I rolled back over onto my back and stared up at the rainy blue night. I closed my eyes as the rain splashed on my face. I stared up through the raindrops and asked God for a miracle.

31

KWAME

I looked all over the apartment complex for my Romeo, but it was as if he had vanished without a trace. The police were out in full force, and from the looks of things, they meant business.

"Don't move. Place your hands in the air and turn around," I heard from a megaphone.

I turned and it seemed like fifty guns were pointed at me. Priest was standing there with all of the boys in blue. He was standing beside a man who appeared to be some high-ranking police officer. I placed my hands above my head, but I didn't turn around.

"Turn around and get on your knees," the megaphone voice said in a threatening tone.

"I'm not turning around and I'm not getting on my knees," I said. "You can see that I don't have any weapons."

"Nobody's gonna shoot you, Kwame," Priest said, walking toward me.

"Hey, that's him," Officer Gripson, the cop who got shot, said as he walked with Priest.

"Nah," Officer Harris, the black guy, said, limping up behind them. "That's not him."

"Where's your friend?" Officer Harris said.

"I don't have any friends," I said calmly. "They are a little overrated if you ask me."

"We're gonna find him, and when we do, it's not gonna be good for him. So do your friend a favor and tell him to turn himself in," Harris said.

"I don't have any friends," I said again, right before three uniformed cops rushed me and slammed me to the ground.

"You're gonna wish you had some friends," Gripson said.

"Am I under arrest?" I asked.

"No," Priest said, "but things will go a lot smoother if you tell us something."

I was glad to see Priest. I knew as long as he was there, I was going to be okay and so was Romeo—whenever we found him.

"I don't know where he is," I said.

"Well, we're gonna be out here all night. Because nobody shoots me and gets away with it. I'm a very patient man, but I'm starting to lose it with you and your little buddies. Now, I'm going to ask you one more time," Gripson said.

"Y'all looking for me," a voice said.

I couldn't believe it. This was not happening. No! This couldn't be happening. I looked up from my predicament on the ground and saw Wicked walking toward the cops.

"I'm the one who shot you," Wicked said, approaching the police with a wide smile on his face.

Both Gripson and Harris looked at each other. Hatred oozed from their pores; they were no doubt thinking about the beat-down Wicked had administered to them. I could literally see the need for revenge in their eyes.

"Is this the guy?" Priest asked.

"Looks like him," Gripson said as he rushed toward Wicked but was held back by one of his fellow officers. "Yeah, that's him."

"Oh, yeah. That's exactly the guy we are looking for," Harris said, licking his lips at the retaliation he had planned for Wicked.

The officers jumped off of me and rushed Wicked. They slammed him down on the concrete and pulled his arms behind his back. A set of handcuffs clicked into place, and he was snatched up by the back of his shirt. Once he was on his feet, he looked at me and gave me a sly smile and a wink.

"Now we're even," he mouthed.

I stood up and watched them take my childhood friend away. He was placed in the back of a police car. I couldn't believe Wicked had come through for us, but I was happy he did.

I watched as the gray and black police cruisers slowly but surely pulled out of the complex.

Priest walked over to me. "Looks like this is going to work out better than any of us anticipated. I guess there is even a little good in the Wicked," he said.

"I guess so," I said as I reached out to shake the lawman's hand. "Thanks, man."

"Don't mention it. Just tell Mr. Romeo to keep his nose clean and to stay out of grown folks' business."

"I will certainly tell him that."

"Well, I need to hurry and get downtown before these guys make a detour and Wicked comes up missing."

"Keep him safe," I said. "He stood tall for my brother and I appreciate that."

Priest nodded and walked off. "I'll get with you guys soon about the money thing. I'm going to make sure Mr. Warship owns up to his end of the deal."

I stayed in the parking lot, standing in the rain. Then something told me to look up. I saw Romeo standing on the roof. He wasn't even hiding anymore. I waved for him to come on down.

Romeo walked up to me on shaky legs. "Where did all the cops go?" he asked, still scared out of his mind.

"It's all good, lil bro," I said, thanking God for sparing my little brother from ever having to see the inside of a jail.

"What happened?" he asked. "Am I going to jail? Where did all of the police officers go?"

"I guess Wicked ain't all that Wicked after all. He paid his debt tonight. We're good," I said with a smile as I rubbed his head and threw my arm around him.

32

KWAME

"Hey, Kwame," Romeo called as we made our way back to the house.

"What's up?"

"We gotta go get Amir."

"Where is he?"

"The cops took him."

We walked over to Amir's house and knocked on the door. Amir's little sister answered. Tears were fresh in her eyes.

"They took Amir to jail for stealing a car," she said. "My mom is trying to get a bail bondsman on the phone."

"Will you tell her to hold off on that for a few?" I said. "I'm going to try something on my end first."

"Okay," she said, then closed the door.

We walked around to Mr. Harold's house. I spoke with him and told him a little white lie that Nana was really upset about Amir being arrested for stealing his car. Mr. Harold jerked his head back and frowned. He would kill a thousand fire ants with his bare hands if that would make Nana smile.

"Let me go find the keys to my pickup," he said, then disappeared back into his house.

Romeo handed me a gun.

"Where did you get this?"

"That's Mr. Harold's gun. It was in his glove compartment."

I took the gun from him. When Mr. Harold came back out, I gave it to him.

"Thank you," he said. "I was worried about this thing. I think I'm going to invest in one of those alarm systems and get rid of these guns. I'm getting too old to be out here busting caps."

We laughed, piled into his pickup, and headed over to the DeKalb Police Department. "I don't make a habit out of lying, but I'll do it this time for Beatrice."

We could hear Amir crying the minute we walked into the building. The police officers never did put him in a cell; they said he was crying so bad that even they felt sorry for him.

Mr. Harold agreed to say that he let Amir borrow his prized Cadillac and that someone had stolen it while it was in his possession. In about another forty-five minutes, we had our boy with us.

Once Amir realized he was a free man, he went back to being Amir.

"Maaaaaan, I'm so happy to see y'all. I was just 'bout to get rowdy up in there. It's a good thing y'all got here when you did. I was just 'bout to whip a little tail. Fools don't know me like that."

"Shut up, boy. I heard you crying from the parking lot," Mr. Harold said.

"Man, Mr. Harold, how could you tell the cops I stole your car?" Amir whined. "I should press charges against you."

"You better be glad I'm even here," Mr. Harold snapped. "Youngin', you done lost what little mind you had when your momma birthed you. Lil ungrateful chump."

"Man, that wasn't my fault. How am I gonna be grateful for you telling a lie and then changing it?" Amir said. "I'm tryna help this clown out," he said, pointing at Romeo.

"It wasn't mine either," Mr. Harold said. "And if you keep on sassing me, I'ma turn around and march my butt right back in that jail and tell them I'm old and senile and the last thing I remember was your lil butt backing out of my driveway without my permission."

Amir put his hands over his mouth, and we all busted out laughing.

"That's more like it," Mr. Harold said, and even he smiled.

"Boy, I feel like a real thug. Done been locked up," Amir said, and he pushed his pants down below his waist and exaggerated his gangster stroll. "Y'all better recognize the fact that I was persecuted because of my political beliefs."

"Boy, do you ever shut up?" Mr. Harold asked.

"How can I run a revolution being quiet?" Amir asked as he threw a closed fist up in the air. "Fight the power."

33

ROMEO

It was almost three o'clock in the morning when Mr. Harold dropped us off. The rain had stopped, and there was a light fog coming from the blacktop. I told Kwame that I was going to walk Amir back to his place.

"That's cool. Try to make it back home without shooting anybody," he said, half joking.

"You don't have to worry about that. I don't ever wanna see another gun in my life," I said. "You can best believe I learned my lesson."

"Good." He smiled. "Amir, you okay?"

"Yeah," Amir said.

"Good. You've always been a good friend to my little brother, and even though what you little clowns did was stupid, I appreciate you having his back. That's big, man."

"You already know . . . that's my dog," Amir said, elbowing me in the ribs.

"I'ma knock your head off if you elbow me like that again," I said.

"Do it," Amir challenged. "I just left the rock, so you really don't wanna test me, Romeo."

Kwame smiled and shook his head. "Y'all be careful. Romeo, come straight home."

"A'ight," I said.

We walked over to Amir's house, both of us lost in our own thoughts. When we made it to his door, he turned to me to say something, but before he could open his mouth, the door flew open and his little sister stood there with open arms. You would've thought he'd just returned home from a two-year tour in Iraq. His mother, who was still up, staring out of the window, screamed and wheeled herself over to Amir. She reached out for a hug, and when he obliged, she wouldn't let go.

"Amirrrrrr," Malaya squealed. "I missed you."

"Aww," I said. "Ain't that sweet."

"Shut up, Rome," Amir said as he was sandwiched between his mother and sister. "We fuss and fight with the best of them, but we are what you might call tight knit up, heh."

I stood there and watched the mighty show of family love and couldn't help but feel a tinge of jealousy. I thought about Pearl and how willing she was to send me away in handcuffs so she could get her money.

"A'ight, man," I said. "I'll holla at you tomorrow."

Amir pried himself away from his family and walked over to me. He motioned with his head for me to step outside. Once we were on the other side of the door, he reached out his hand. "You came for me, dog. You didn't leave me in there."

"Did you think I would?"

"To be honest with you, Rome, I didn't know what to

think. I was scared, man. That jail life is not the life I had planned for myself."

"I hear you," I said, thinking back to the conversation I had had with Ngiai's stepdad.

"But something told me I was going to be a'ight. I just knew God wasn't going to do me like that."

"Wicked took the fall for the shooting," I said. "I can't believe he confessed."

"That's the least he could do. Everybody round here knows he let Kwame go to jail behind his foolishness. I guess he lifted up that fat gut and found a conscience."

"Well, I'm glad he did. Kwame could handle anything, but, man, I think I would've lost my mind if I had to go to jail. The police came for me and I ran. I was on top of the C building, and all kinds of thoughts were running through my head. I looked down and saw them taking you, and I swear I wanted to end it all right there on the spot. For the first time in my life, I seriously contemplated suicide."

"Boy, are you crazy? Black folk don't kill themselves. That for rich white people. We are used to dealing with crap."

I chuckled and reached out and patted my boy on the shoulders. "But I'm glad I didn't because we have plans to be somebody."

"Rome," Amir said with a tear starting in the corner of his eye. "When I was in that car riding to jail, I thought about my dad. I never met the man. He's been locked up all of my life. I only know him through his letters, but I like to think that we are pretty close. He was sent to jail about five months before I was born for trying to assassinate the president. They gave him fifty years. I never told anybody why he was locked up, because that just sounds crazy for a poor black man to try to kill the president, but that's what he did. Anyway, when I was in those handcuffs, I thought about what he said to me in one of his letters. He told me to never let the authorities put those chains on your wrist. He said having those chains on your wrist takes some of your soul away. He said the more you had chains on you, the less of a man you become and more of an animal, because you were being controlled by a man. Does that make sense to you, Rome?"

I nodded.

"Rome," Amir said, wiping his tears away. "I'm not an animal. I was just being a friend."

"I know, bro. I know. And I couldn't think of a better one. You my dog."

"Thanks for coming to get me, man."

"You already know. Besides, if you go to jail, who's going to lead the revolution?"

Amir smiled. "Fight the power," he said, then threw his fist in the air. "I'm going to the house to write Dad a letter, bro. I'll holla at you tomorrow."

"A'ight," I said, and we shared a brotherly hug.

I walked back to my apartment on a slow stroll. A million and one thoughts were racing through my head. I looked around the apartment complex and shook my head at just how close I had come to having it all taken away. I walked a little farther and then stopped and stared at the playground.

"Wow," was all I could say as I witnessed firsthand how the streets replenished themselves with new hustlers. It appeared one of Wicked's flunkies had promoted himself, because he was leaning on Wicked's car doing the business of the Wicked. I shook my head and kept walking. Just another night in the Village.

EPILOGUE
ROMEO

Three months later

All of the paperwork had been signed, and we moved out of the Village. Nana was the custodian of all the funds that had been handed over. I really wanted her to buy a big pretty house out in Ngiai's neighborhood, but she wouldn't hear any of it.

"You going off to college and Kwame is too. So what makes you think I want some big old house just for me and Pearl?"

As usual, she got her way. The first thing we purchased with Dirty Harry's money was a classy three-bedroom ranch-style house in historical Decatur. The house was at the end of a cul-de-sac, and it sported its very own two-car garage. Inside the garage was a brand-new Infinity SUV, which we would use to transport Nana around. The MARTA passes were a thing of the past. Nana's bedroom was the house's greatest asset. Built-in bookcases, custom shutters, and hardwood floors. She had her very own fireplace, which was situated so that you could enjoy it while in the bathroom or the bedroom. And speaking of the bathroom, it was straight out of a magazine. Travertine floors and walls, marble countertops, and two huge sinks. The Jacuzzi bathtub was so big it looked like a small swimming pool. Every time she walked into that room, I could see a smile on her face. And to me, seeing her like that was absolutely priceless and worth every single event that had transpired leading up to it.

Pearl agreed to check herself into a mental hospital. We found an in-patient facility that wasn't too far from the house, and she was working hard to get herself back to the mother she wants to be. She kept insisting that I call her "Mom," and whenever I slipped up, she acted like she was going to cry. Calling her Mom was hard for me, though, especially since she had been so willing to send me off to the cops just so she could get her money. The only thing that allowed me to forgive her was her illness.

Ngiai knocked on our door and Nana let her in.

"Whoooooweee," Ngiai said. "What are you getting all jazzy for?"

"Got a hot date," Nana said with a smile.

"Nana," I said. "You told me you were going—"

"Hush, boy," she said, then disappeared back into her huge master suite.

"Don't hate," Ngiai said as she walked past me and into the living room.

"Be quiet," I said, not sure how I was feeling about my grandmother getting dolled up and going God knows where.

"I love this house," Ngiai said. "It's so classy and quaint." She stopped and looked at me. "Guess what?"

"You forgive me?" I said with a smile.

"Nope."

"Okay, then, what?"

"I'm going to the University of South Carolina."

"Really?"

"Yeah. Now, I might forgive you if you tell me you're coming with me."

"But I was kind of leaning toward UGA," I said.

"Well, lean a little farther east," she said.

"I don't know. That's a nice little hump for Nana to have to make."

"Boy, shut up. Like Nana got time to be coming to your games. Mr. Harold got that on lockdown. He gonna be moving in here soon. Don't act like you don't know," Ngiai said with a sly smile.

"Stop playing," I said with a frown, trying not to hear what she was talking about.

"Whatever. Let Nana get her mack on. She deserves to be happy, and Mr. Harold got that nose wide open," Ngiai said. "He's outside now smiling and listening to love songs. Playing that Luther to get his game right."

"Get out," I said.

She fanned me off and walked into the living room, where my brother and his girlfriend, Kelli, were. They were wrapped up in some twisted cuddling position on the sofa.

"Hey, Kwame, hey, Kelli," she said as she plopped down on the love seat.

"What's up, baby girl?" Kwame said.

"Hi, Ngiai," Kelli said.

"Kwame, can you please tell your knuckle-headed brother that he needs to go to the University of South Carolina?"

"Romeo, you need to go to the University of South Carolina," he said, nestling himself back into Kelli's arms.

"Man." Ngiai sucked her teeth at Kwame's lack of help. "Kelli, will you tell this boy he better come to South Carolina or he's gonna mess around and miss out on a good thing here?"

"Is that where you're going?" Kelli asked.

"Yeah, and I'm tryna get this one here to not send me over there with all those fine men by my lonesome," Ngiai said with a pouty face.

"Whatever, you ain't giving 'em none," I said.

"How do you know what I'm going to do?"

"You better not give nobody none," I said.

"Now, why is sex the first thing to pop into your pea-size brain?" Ngiai said. "That's the reason why I'm not your girlfriend right now."

"Whatever," I said. "You know you love me."

"Romeo, USC might not be a bad place for you," Kwame said, untangling himself from Kelli. He sat up. "I've been thinking about that. They are in your top three, right?"

"Yep," I said. "UGA and Tennessee are the other two."

"Well, go to South Carolina, man. I really need for you to get away from Georgia, but I don't need you to be too far away, and they are saying you will have a chance to start."

My brother had never asked me for anything. And lately he'd been selling me on going to Carolina. I think he felt that he owed the school something after leaving them hanging while he took care of his troubles.

"They want me to go to receiver but I'm a quarterback," I said. "If they let me play quarterback, then I'll go."

Kwame smiled and picked up the telephone. He dialed a few numbers, then spoke. "Coach Spurrier, Kwame Braxton here," he said as he hit the speaker phone button.

"Hey, Kwame," Coach Spurrier said with his high-pitched voice. "How you doing, my friend? That scholarship is still yours if you want it."

"I appreciate that, Coach, but I'm calling about Romeo."

"We want him too. Bad. We need him. If we can get both of you guys, I think I might pass out," Coach said.

"Well, he wants to play quarterback, but he said you guys wanna use him at receiver. That's the only holdup."

"Yeah, we wanna use him as receiver just to get him on the field, but make no mistake about it—he's my quarterback. I have a senior now who'll be a top-ten pick in this year's NFL draft, so I can't bench him, but I need Romeo on the field. Next year, he'll have a chance to compete for the number-one spot at the quarterback position."

"Hey, Coach," I said. "This is Romeo."

"Hey there, big guy. You ready to be a Gamecock?"

I paused and thought about what I had just heard. "I think so," I said.

Ngiai started clapping and jumped up and hugged my neck.

"Is this a verbal commitment?" Coach Spurrier said.

"Yes, sir," I said. "I'm coming."

"Well, good. One down, one to go. Kwame, what are you going to do?"

"Coach," Kwame said. "I have a lot of work to do right here in my city. I think Romeo can hold it down."

"Well, I'll hold your spot for as long as I can. If you change your mind, you have the number," he said.

"Thanks, Coach," Kwame said.

"Romeo, I'll see you in about two months. Come ready to work, and welcome to the Gamecock family."

"Thanks, Coach," I said. "I'll see you soon."

Kwame hung up the phone and we shared a good, brotherly hug.

"What are you gonna do?" I asked.

"I'm going to take some classes at Georgia Perimeter and try to start a foundation."

"So are you done with football?"

"Playing, yes," Kwame said. "But I'm sure I'll be involved some kind of way."

The doorbell rang and he released me so that I could go and answer the door.

Amir walked in wearing a University of Georgia hat, shirt, sweatpants, and a pair of UGA shades.

"I guess we know where you're going to school," Ngiai said. "I didn't know they had special education classes down at UGA."

"Shut up, Ngiai. The last thing you need before you go to freshman orientation is a black eye," Amir said.

"How you gonna reach my eyes? On your tippy toes?" Ngiai said.

"That's why Romeo gonna leave your little bougie butt. Me and my dog gonna be down in Athens. We gonna be getting all the honeys. White girls, Asian girls, black girls, green girls. We ain't even gonna discriminate," Amir said, making kissing motions to every imaginable girl he called out.

"Not," Ngiai teased. "He's coming with me to the University of South Carolina."

Amir's eyes almost popped out of his head. "What!" he said, looking at me like I was Judas.

I nodded to confirm.

"Awww, hell no," he yelled.

"Amir," Nana called out. "Are you using bad language in my house?"

"No, ma'am," he said. "I said hello."

"Alright, boy," she said.

"Man." He turned back to me. "You done got me locked up, almost killed by some dirty cops, and now you gonna bail on me. You about the foulest dude I know."

"Aw, don't worry about it, Amir," Kelli said. "You can always ride the three hours down there to see your man."

"First of all, Kelli, Romeo is not my man. I don't get down like that, so if that's what you're implying, then you need to stop. And forget Romeo. He ain't nothing but a sellout. Bulldogs will whip up on a Gamecock any day of the week," Amir said, popping his shirt.

The doorbell rang again and Amir stomped away to get it.

"Man, why are you answering other people's doors?" Ngiai said.

"Shut up," Amir said, walking back into the living room. "Mr. Harold, you sharp, man."

"How y'all young people doing?" Mr. Harold said, standing there in a three-piece suit with a derby brim in his hand.

"We're good," everyone said.

Nana walked in all dressed up in her Sunday best.

"Where y'all going?" I asked.

"To see a man about a mule. Now mind your business," Nana said. "Hey, Amir. Amir, if I hear you cuss one more time in my house, I'm going to whip your butt. And when are you going home?"

"I just got here," he said.

"Oh, you're here so much I thought you moved in," Nana said. "We're going to see that stage play *The Color Purple*. The food is in the oven."

"Look at cha, house so big you don't know who's up in here. Gone, Queen Nana," Amir said.

"Y'all young people have a good afternoon, now," Mr. Harold said.

"Bye," we all said.

"Mr. Harold," I said, pointing a warning finger at him.

He looked at me after Nana had walked by and gave me that crooked and exaggerated winking of his eye.

The phone rang and I answered it.

"You have a collect call from an inmate at the DeKalb County Jail. To accept the call, press one."

I pressed the number one.

"Wicked," I said. "What's good?"

"Hey, boy. How you doing?"

"I'm good. The gang's all here, so I'ma put you on speaker phone."

"What's up, bro?" Kwame said.

"I'm good. I'm about ready to get on down the road, man. This jail thing ain't fit for roaches."

"How much time they give you?" Kwame asked.

"Thanks to you and that sexy lawyer Mrs. Ross, I got two years. I was looking at a lot more than that, but she's the bomb and got them all messed up. They couldn't go very far, because they didn't want some of their dirt to come out, so we did a little plea deal. It's all good."

"Cool. She's a very good lawyer," Kwame said.

"Yeah, man. When I'm done with this, they ain't ever got to worry about seeing my sexy butt no more."

"Stop lying. All convicts say that when they locked up," Amir said. "What you gonna do next, join the Muslims?"

"Who is that? Amir?" Wicked asked.

"That's right, punk. Say something," Amir said, acting brave.

"You know the first thing I'ma do when I get out, Amir?"

"What? Get a thirty-piece dinner from KFC?" Amir said. "And clog up some more of your arteries?"

"Nah. I'ma slap the taste out of your mouth," Wicked said.

"Yeah, yeah, yeah. I'm shaking over here, man," Amir said. "You should see."

"Yo, Wicked," I said. "Thanks again for what you did, dude. That was real."

"Don't sweat it, Romeo. Besides, you gotta go get that NFL money. And I want the entire signing bonus."

"I don't know about the whole signing bonus, but I got you," I said.

"Man," Wicked said. "You must be my dog because real Gs take care of real Gs. Check this out, Kwame. I had a dream last night that I was still playing football. I asked Mrs. Ross to look into finding a program that will allow me to get back at it when I get out."

"Oh, yeah," Kwame said, smiling. "What school you talking about?"

Wicked yelled at the top of his lungs, "Bulldogs, baby."

"No," Amir screamed. "Oh, God, say it ain't so."

"Shut up, midget, and you already know I expect you to write all of my papers," Wicked said.

"You'll be on criminal and academic probation if you

think I'm doing one sentence for you," Amir said, holding his ground.

"Yeah, okay, I'll see if you wanna still talk that crap when I get home."

"I'll be right here waiting on you," Amir said. "Hey, Wicked."

"What?"

"On the real, man. Get up outta there and do something with your life, man. Our people are strong and smart. We are not wild animals, so we are not meant to be held in cages. You know I like to mess with you, but I always thought you were smart. Use that head for more than a hat rack. And if you do come down to UGA, I'd gladly help you with your papers."

"I appreciate that, midget. On the real, that's the nicest thing anyone ever said to me," Wicked said, and even over the phone, I could hear the emotion in his voice.

There was a clicking sound, and that meant the call was coming to an end.

"Hey, y'all, stay up," Wicked said. "They 'bout to cut me off."

"We love you, Wicked," Ngiai and Kelli said.

"Aww, damn," Wicked said. "Y'all ain't 'bout to have me up in here crying."

"Take care, bro," Kwame said. "You are about as real as they come."

"I try. Lord knows I do," Wicked said before the line went dead.

We hung up the phone with Wicked and sat around talking about our future plans.

TWO THE HARD WAY

Travis Hunter

ABOUT THIS GUIDE

The following questions are intended to
enhance your group's reading of
TWO THE HARD WAY.

DISCUSSION QUESTIONS

1. Romeo grew up in a rough environment, yet he still managed to be a good kid and a good student. Do you think the challenges he faced made him a stronger person or forced him to have to grow up too quickly?

2. Romeo was a star athlete and seemed to receive preferential treatment from his coach, yet he was treated the exact opposite by the principal of the school. Why do you think that happened?

3. Romeo is ready to have sex, yet his girlfriend, Ngiai, is not. Why do you think there is so much pressure put on young men to rush into sex?

4. Amir is trying to change his environment but gets little support from the very people he's trying to help. Do you think people can find comfort in their misery?

5. Kwame threw away a bright future by hanging with the wrong person, yet he didn't snitch. Why do you think our young people consider "keeping it real" more important than protecting their own futures?

6. Kwame accepted money from Wicked even though he despised where it came from. Do you blame him?

7. Nana raised her grandkids to be respectful and law-abiding young men, yet both of them ended up in trouble. Why do you think some "good" kids get into trouble?

8. Pearl's mental illness seems to bring the family a sense of shame. Why do you think there is so much stigma about mental illness in the African-American community?

9. Wicked ended up taking the rap to save Romeo's future. Do you think it was guilt, or was he trying to save Romeo from the same fate as his older brother?

10. Kwame had an opportunity to go off to college and play with his brother, yet he decided to stay home and try to help his community. Do you think prison was a blessing in disguise?

11. Who do you think can benefit most from this novel?

Don't miss Franky's story in

At the Crossroads

Coming in December 2010 from Dafina Books

Turn the page for an excerpt from *At the Crossroads*. . . .

Franklin "Franky" Bourgeois was fast asleep in his bed when he was startled awake by the sound of gunshots. He jumped up and ran out of his room to make sure his cousins, Nigel and Rico, were alright. Nigel was sleeping peacefully, as if he were lying out on a beach somewhere. Rico wasn't in his room, but he was always out in the street at all times of night. Franky walked back to his room and sat on the bed.

Pow. Pow. Pow.

He heard the shots again, but this time from a different type of gun. He heard someone running in the backyard, right outside of his window. Then, all of a sudden, as if he were watching a low-budget action film, someone leaped through his open bedroom window. He jumped up, ready to fight.

The boy, who was about his age, give or take a year or two, held his hands up to his mouth, signaling for Franky to be quiet.

"Man, what the—" Franky began, then lowered his voice. "What do you think you are doing?"

"Please, man," the boy said, on the verge of tears. "These dudes out there tryna kill me."

"Kill you?"

"Yes. Please, man," the boy pleaded.

"I don't know anything about that, but you gonna have to get out of here," Franky said, walking over to his bedroom door. "You can go back out of that window or use the door, but you need to leave right now."

"Pleaseeeeee, man. I'm begging you. I didn't do nothing, man. I'm not a thief or anything like that, man. I work every day." Real tears started to roll down his cheeks. "I don't wanna die, man. My momma . . . ," he said, then dropped his head.

Franky didn't respond. He stood at the door, watching the boy.

The boy must've read the hesitation in Franky's eyes because he started pulling wads of money from both pockets. "Here, I'll pay you."

Desperation was oozing out of the boy's eyes. Something told Franky that the boy was okay, yet he was still weary. People played all kinds of games in the hood. This wasn't some nice suburban area of Atlanta where you could give someone the benefit of the doubt. He cursed himself for leaving his window up, but the heat in the house was unbearable.

"Take it. Here, take it. Just let me stay here for a few more minutes," the boy said in a whisper.

Franky heard footsteps and some people talking outside the window.

"Where that fool go?"

"I don't know. He gotta be round here somewhere."

The boy looked at Franky and held up his hands as if he were praying.

"Frankyyyy," one of the voices called from the outside.

"Yeah," Franky said, walking over to the window, feigning sleep. "What's up?"

"You hear anything back here?"

Franky recognized the voice of a guy from the neighborhood that everyone called Stick. Stick was an older guy, at least thirty-five years old, who spent his time running around the hood with teenagers. He still lived with his mother and was always running some hustle.

"Nah," Franky said, all of a sudden feeling sorry for the guy who was hiding behind him on the floor. "Is that you out here shooting?"

"Yeah, came up on a lil lick, but the fool got away. He must be a track star, 'cause that fool was moving. Messed up my night, 'cause I need that money."

"Yeah, well, I'm sorry I couldn't help you, Stick," Franky said. "And use some silencers the next time. I gotta go to school in the morning."

"School?" Stick said with a frown. "You going lame on me?"

"Yeah," Franky said.

"A'ight, lil homie," Stick said. "Take your lame tail back to bed."

"You see him?" Rico said as he approached Stick from the opposite direction. "Franky, you hear anybody back here?"

"Nope," Franky said, disappointed but not surprised to see that his cousin was involved in this little scheme.

"A'ight, let's walk up this way, Stick," Rico said with a big smile on his face, as if they were playing a game of hide-and-go-seek. "I know that fool can't be too far away, ya heard?"

Franky closed the window and walked back over to his bed. He sat down and sighed.

"Thanks, man," the boy said. "Those dudes are crazy."

"You right about that," Franky said.

"May I use your phone? I dropped mine when I was running."

"We don't have a phone, whoadie."

The boy sighed and rubbed his hands over his face as if the harder he rubbed, the quicker he could come up with a solution to his current predicament.

"Here," the boy said, handing Franky the money. "A deal is a deal. You saved my life."

"What are you gonna do? You can't stay here."

"I know," the boy said. "Can you give me a little time to figure something out?"

"Might as well. You're here," Franky said with a hunch of his shoulders. "But one of those dudes . . . ," Franky started, but caught himself. He didn't know this guy and he didn't want him returning with the police to take Rico away.

The boy sat in silence for a few minutes before Franky spoke. "Where did you get all of this money from?"

"I work," the boy said. "I was over here trying to buy this car, but the guy kept giving me the runaround. Now that I think about it, it was a hustle the whole time." The boy shook his head. "No wonder they kept saying bring cash. Cash only. Cash only."

Franky knew exactly the hustle he was referring to. Take a picture of a nice car—a Dodge Charger, Chevrolet Impala, or something like that—post it on a Web site that sells cars, and when the person comes to test-drive it, the goons pop out. Some guys used a girl to distract the guy, and then they would take his money.

Franky held the guy's money in his hand. He leaned over so he could use the streetlight for illumination and counted the bills. He counted out three thousand dollars.

"It's like eleven o'clock at night. Why would you come to buy a car this time of night, in this neighborhood? Do you have a death wish? Or maybe you just wanna be robbed."

"Nah. I just got off work. I jumped straight on the MARTA," the boy said, shaking his head. "Wow. I could be dead right now."

"Yes, you could," Franky said, handing the boy back his money and standing up. "But you are not, so go home."

The boy held his hand up and refused the money.

"Here," Franky said, pushing the money at his chest. "Take your money."

The boy took a deep breath, then reached for his cash.

"Just be a little more careful the next time," Franky said.

"Man, can I give you some of it? You don't know what you did for me."

"Yes, I do," Franky said, walking out of the room and leading the guy to the front door. "But I would want somebody to do the same thing for me. Take care, whoadie."

"Man," the boy said, looking around when Franky opened the front door. "My name is Davante. I'm not going to forget this. I have to give you something. Here," he said, handing Franky about five or six hundred-dollar bills.

"Thanks," Franky said as he took the money.

"I'ma come back by here and . . . I don't know what I'm going to do, but I wanna let you know I appreciate this."

"Don't sweat it, man," Franky said.

Davante reached out his hand, and Franky shook it. "Be careful out there, ya heard?"

"Yeah," Devante said as he looked around one last time, then took off running.

Franky watched him as he ran down the sidewalk without looking back.